Magical Stories

For 6 Year olds

Helen Paiba was one of the most committed, knowledgeable and acclaimed children's booksellers in Britain. For more than twenty years she owned and ran the Children's Bookshop in Muswell Hill, London, which under her guidance gained a superb reputation for its range of children's books and for the advice available to its customers.

Helen was also involved with the Booksellers Association for many years and served on both its Children's Bookselling Group and the Trade Practices Committee.

In 1995 she was given honorary life membership of the Booksellers Association of Great Britain and Ireland in recognition of her outstanding services to the association and to the book trade. In the same year the Children's Book Circle (sponsored by Books for Children) honoured her with the Eleanor Farjeon Award, given for distinguished service to the world of children's books.

Books in this series

Animal Stories for 5 Year Olds
Animal Stories for 6 Year Olds

Bedtime Stories for 5 Year Olds
Bedtime Stories for 6 Year Olds

Funny Stories for 5 Year Olds
Funny Stories for 6 Year Olds
Funny Stories for 7 Year Olds
Funny Stories for 8 Year Olds

Magical Stories for 5 Year Olds
Magical Stories for 6 Year Olds

Scary Stories for 7 Year Olds

Magical Stories

For **6** year olds

Chosen by Helen Paiba

Illustrated by Anthony Lewis

MACMILLAN CHILDREN'S BOOKS

For Sarah Davies, my editor, with many thanks

First published 1999 by Macmillan Children's Books

This edition published 2016 by Macmillan Children's Books
an imprint of Pan Macmillan
20 New Wharf Road, London N1 9RR
Associated companies throughout the world
www.panmacmillan.com

ISBN 978-1-5098-0616-4

7 9 8 6

A CIP catalogue record for this book is available from
the British Library.

Typeset by SX Composing DTP, Rayleigh, Essex
Printed and bound by CPI Group (UK) Ltd, Croydon CR0 4YY

Contents

The Sandboat

Berlie Doherty

Joe filled two buckets with wet sand and carried them up to where his mum and dad were sitting in their stripy deckchairs.

"Cover your arms up, Joe," his mum said. "Don't you go and get sunburnt." She was shiny with suntan oil, like a big pink dolphin.

"Don't wander off," his dad said, "or you'll get lost." He took his shoes and socks off and wiggled

1

his toes about like crabs in the sand.

Joe fetched some more wet sand and tipped it out of the buckets.

"Don't tip that sand out near me," Mum said. "It'll get in my eyes."

Dad said: "Don't get it in your hair, Joe, or we'll have to bath you tonight."

Joe fetched more sand and tipped it out.

"Don't bring any more of that wet sand over here," his mum said.

"You've got enough," said Dad.

"Leave some for other people," his mum said.

Joe stood up. The tide was

coming in, like a long brown snuffling creature. He ran down with his buckets and filled them up again. He stood by his pile and dolloped the new sand down.

"Stop chucking sand about," his mum said. She closed her eyes and yawned.

Joe picked up his red spade and dug a hollow in the middle of the sand pile. He patted the sides.

"Don't get your hands muddy," Dad said, half asleep.

Joe dug and dug and built and built. He wasn't sure what he was making, except that it had a rounded front and a hollow inside with a little built-up bit like a seat,

and it was long. The sun grew high and hot. The sea snuffled nearer and nearer.

"Don't get wet," Mum murmured, and fell fast asleep.

Dad snored. "Don't . . ." he rumbled.

All of a sudden Joe knew what he was building. It was a boat. It was definitely a boat. He was excited now. He ran from side to side and all around it, adding a bit more sand, patting the sides, rubbing them to make them round. It was a beautiful boat. He stuck a long white gull's feather on the front bit, the prow. He lay flat on his belly and blew the feather and it fluttered, just like a flag.

He stuck shells along the sides in a long line. Then he stood up. The brown snuffly tide was almost in. He climbed into his sandboat and sat on the seat that was only just big enough for him, and waited.

Slowly the sea crept round the

boat. Joe watched the water trickle as far as Dad's bare toes, but it didn't wake him up. It dribbled round Mum's bag of sandwiches, but it didn't wake her up. Joe wriggled in his sandy seat. The sea was all around him.

And then Joe's boat began to move. At first it was just a little rocking movement, and then it seemed to lift and sway like a swing, gently up, gently down, and then it was floating. It was really floating. The white feather fluttered like a real flag.

Joe sailed past the men and women and dogs who were paddling round him. He sailed

past the children who were
jumping up and down and
splashing and shrieking. He sailed
past the bobbing heads of all the
swimmers, past them, past them
all, out to sea. He trailed his
hands over the edge and felt the
waves slapping his fingers. He
could feel the spray tickling his
cheeks. He laughed out loud, and
high above him the seagulls
laughed too.

He looked over his shoulder and
saw, far behind him, the tiny
figures on the beach. He could just
see Mum and Dad, fast asleep in
their deckchairs.

Shoals of fishes drifted round

him, flashing like stars in the water. The waves sparkled in the sunlight. When he closed his eyes he could hear the whales singing to each other, miles and miles below him. He sang back to them, as loud as he could, at the top of his voice, louder than he'd ever sung in his life before. A dolphin jumped out of the water and clapped its fins at him.

Far away he could see a huge ship, like a castle in the water. It was an ocean liner. It loomed up to him, rocking his little sandboat with the giant white waves it made. His dolphin leapt in the air with excitement. *Booom!* went the ship's loud hooter. "Tooot!" shouted Joe. "Toooot!" The captain came on deck and saluted him. Joe stood up in his sandboat and saluted back.

"That's a fine craft you have, Captain!" the captain shouted.

"Thank you, Captain," shouted Joe. He felt as round as an egg with pride.

"Going far?" the captain shouted.

"Miles!" Joe shouted back. "Are you going far?"

"Australia!" said the captain.

"Don't get lost!" Joe shouted, and he and the captain laughed.

"I might!" said the captain. "It's a long way to Australia!"

"You can borrow my dolphin if you like," said Joe, and his dolphin flicked its tail and swam off towards the liner, to lead it all the way to Australia.

Joe waved to the liner till it was out of sight. He looked over the side of his boat, and saw the fishes swimming like seagulls in the water. He looked up and saw the seagulls floating like fishes in the sky.

All of a sudden his boat gave a little soft bump, and Joe realized that he had landed on the shore. The tide was trickling away from him, like a long snuffling creature scurrying back home. It whispered away like smoke. Joe climbed out of his boat. It was strange to be standing still again, on dry land.

Mum and Dad were just beginning to wake up.

"I hope you didn't wander off," said Dad.

"I hope you haven't eaten the sandwiches," said Mum. She looked in her bag. "Just look at them. They're wet!"

"Why didn't you tell us the tide was coming in?" said Dad.

"We could have floated away on our deckchairs," said Mum.

And Joe smiled to himself, and didn't say a word.

The Three Wishes

Rose Impey

One night a man and his wife were sitting before their fire, talking, cosy-like. She was a good wife and he was a good man so they were passing happy, most of the time. But now and again the pair of them couldn't help feeling just a bit envious of their neighbours, who were richer than them.

"It doesn't seem fair," said the wife.

"It certainly don't," said her husband.

"Now, if I had a wish," said she, "I know just what I'd do with it. Ooh, I'd be happier than all of 'em."

"And me," said the man. "Pity there isn't such a thing as a fairy, right here, this minute."

And suddenly there was, right there, that minute, in their own kitchen. All shining and smiling.

"You can have three wishes," the fairy told them, "but take care – once they're gone, that's it, there'll be no more." And then she disappeared. She was very businesslike.

Well, the couple were amazed. They felt as if they had their heads on back to front.

"Whatever d'you make of that?" said he.

"I'll tell you what I make of it," said she. "I know fine well what I'll wish for – not that I'm wishing yet," she said, quick as a flash, in case the fairy was listening, "but, if I *were*, I should want to be handsome, rich and famous."

"Where's the use in that?" said he. "That won't stop you being sick and miserable or dying young. Far better be healthy and hopeful and live to be a hundred."

"And how would that help, if you

15

were poor and hungry in the meantime?" said she. "Just prolonging the misery, in my opinion."

Well, her husband had to agree with that.

"Hmmm," said he. "This is going to need some thinking about. I reckon we'd best go to bed and sleep on it. We'll be wiser in the morning than the evening."

"True enough," said his wife.

But the fire was still burning up brightly, so they sat on a little longer, talking things over, cosy-like.

They were feeling that happy.

"It'd be a waste to leave this nice

fire," said the man.

"It does seem a pity, though," said she, "we've nowt to cook on it. I wish we had a dozen sausages for our supper."

Uh, oh! No sooner said than done.

Down the chimney fell a long chain of sausages and landed at their feet. And that was one wish gone.

The man was flummoxed. He could hardly speak for rage.

"A dozen sausages! What a witless woman is my wife. Of all the hare-brained individuals . . . I wish the dozen sausages were stuck on the end of your nose,

17

you nincompoop.

Uh, oh! No sooner said than done.

The sausages leapt up onto the end of the wife's nose and hung there like an elephant's trunk. And that was two wishes gone.

"Oh, flipping heck, what have you done to me!" said she. She took hold of the sausages and tried to get them off. She pulled and pummelled them, she twisted and turned them, but they wouldn't budge. In sheer temper she jumped out of her chair, stepped on the end of them and almost tripped up. By now she was fizzing mad!

Her husband sat there open-mouthed, just watching.

"Don't sit there gawping, you owl, do something, for goodness sake," she cried.

So then the husband tried too. He grabbed hold of the sausages and he pulled and he pulled. It was a regular tug-of-war. But the sausages just stretched longer and longer and longer. When he finally let go they sprang back like a piece of elastic, boxing his wife round the ears – biff! biff! biff! Then they hung down, long and floppy again.

"Oh, what a wretched woman I am," she began to cry. "Whatever

will I do?" And her tears ran down
the sausages.

"Don't fret," said he. "I know just
what to do. We must use our last
wish to make ourselves very rich.
Then I shall have the smartest
gold case in the world made for
you to wear over the sausages.

Maybe a matching crown. You'll
look very grand."

"Are you a complete idiot?" said
the wife. "Have you totally lost
your senses? D'you suppose I want
to spend the rest of my days
trailing sausages on the end of my
nose? You must have a screw loose.
I want that last wish to get rid of
these sausages," she said, "or . . . I
shall throw myself out of the
window."

And to show she meant it, she
rushed across the room, threw
open the window and jumped up
on the window sill.

Then her husband couldn't help
but smile. The sight of his poor

21

wife, standing on the window sill with a string of sausages hanging from her nose, was such a comical sight. And, after all, they were still sitting downstairs, so she hardly had far to jump.

But he was a bit of a tease and he couldn't resist winding her up one last time.

"Of course, my dear, you must do whatever you think best, but it does seem a pity, knowing as how you wanted to be famous and all that. And truly, the more I look at it, the more it grows on me. I'm really beginning to think as it suits you."

"Suits me? A nose as long as a

skipping rope? I should be tripping over it every way I turned," she cried.

"Happen you could wrap it round your neck, lovely, then it'd serve as a scarf an'all," he said, trying to be helpful.

At this, his wife was fit to explode, but the man couldn't keep it up a minute longer. He started to grin, so he got up and helped her off the ledge. For he did truly love her.

"I wish my wife could have her nose back to normal," he said.

Da daa! No sooner said than done.

The sausages fell to the floor and

coiled themselves up like a pet snake.

"Well, some good's come of the bad," said she, "at least we still have the sausages."

"I'll build up the fire," said he.

"I'll put on the pan," said she.

"What a good idea," said he.

So that's what they did.

The pair of them sat late into the night, frying sausages and toasting their toes before the fire, and talking, cosy-like.

The Boy Who Wasn't Bad Enough

Lance Salway

$\mathcal{A}$ long time ago, in a far country, there lived a boy called Claud who was so bad that people both far and near had heard of his naughtiness. His mother and father loved him dearly, and so did his brothers and sisters, but even they became angry at the tricks he played on

25

them and the mischief that he caused by his bad behaviour.

Once, when his grandmother came to stay, Claud put a big, fat frog in her bed. Once, when the teacher wasn't looking, he changed the hands on the school clock so that the children were sent home two hours early. And once, when Claud was feeling especially bad, he cut his mother's washing line so that the clean clothes fell into the mud, and he poured a bottle of ink over the head of his eldest sister, and he locked his two young brothers into a cupboard and threw the key down a well. And, as if that wasn't bad enough, he climbed to the top of the tallest tree in the garden and tied his father's best shirt to the topmost branch so that it waved in the wind like a flag.

His parents and his brothers and sisters did all they could to stop Claud's mischief and to make him a better boy. They sent him to bed without any supper, but that didn't make any difference. They wouldn't let him go to the circus when it came to the town, but that didn't make any difference. They wouldn't let him go out to play with his friends, but that didn't make any difference either because Claud hadn't any friends.

All the other boys and girls of the town were much too frightened to play with him and, in any case, their parents wouldn't let them. But Claud didn't mind. He liked to play tricks on people and he enjoyed being as bad as possible. And he laughed when his parents became cross or his brothers and sisters cried because he liked to see how angry they would get when he was naughty.

"What *are* we to do with you?" sighed his mother. "We've tried everything we can think of to stop you being naughty. And it hasn't made any difference at all."

"But I enjoy being bad," said

28

Claud, and he pushed his youngest sister so hard that she fell on the floor with a thump.

Everybody in the town had heard of Claud's naughtiness, and it wasn't long before the news spread to the next town and the next until everyone had heard that Claud was the naughtiest boy in the land. The king and queen had heard of Claud's naughtiness. And even the Chief Witch, who was the oldest and the ugliest and the most wicked witch in the kingdom, had heard of him too.

One day, the Chief Witch came to visit Claud's parents. They were very frightened when they saw her

but Claud was overjoyed,
especially when she told him that
if he promised to be very bad
indeed she would allow him to ride
on her broomstick.

"I believe your son is the
naughtiest boy in the whole
country," she said to Claud's
father.

"He is," he replied sadly.

"Good!" said the Witch. "I would
like him to join my school for bad
children. We are always looking
for clever children to train as
witches and wizards. And the
naughtier they are, the better."

Claud was very pleased when he
heard of the Witch's plan and he

begged his parents to allow him to go to her school.

"At least we'd have some peace," said his mother. "Yes, you may as well go, if it will make you happy."

"Oh, it will, it will!" shouted Claud, and he rushed upstairs to get ready for the journey. And so, a few days later, the Chief Witch called again on her broomstick to take Claud to her school. He said goodbye to his parents and his brothers and sisters and climbed onto the broomstick behind her. He couldn't wave to his family but he smiled happily at them as he flew away on the long journey to school, clutching the broomstick with one hand and holding his suitcase with the other.

Everybody was pleased to see him go. The people of the town were pleased. Claud's brothers and sisters were pleased.

"Now we can enjoy ourselves," they said. "Claud won't be here to play tricks on us now."

Even his mother and father were pleased. "He'll be happy with the Witch," they said. "He can be as bad as he likes now."

But, as time passed, they found that they all missed Claud.

"It was much more fun when he was here," complained his brothers and sisters. "We never knew what would happen next."

Claud's mother and father, too, began to wish that he had never gone away. Even though he was such a bad boy they loved him dearly and wished that they had never allowed the Chief Witch to take him to school. And the people of the town wished that Claud would come back.

"There was never a dull moment when Claud was here," they sighed. "Now, nothing ever happens in our town."

As the weeks passed, Claud's family missed him more and more.

"Perhaps he'll come back to visit us," his mother said.

But the summer ended and autumn passed and then winter came but still there was no visit from Claud.

"He'll never come back," said his father sadly.

And then, on a cold night in the middle of winter, they heard a faint knock on the front door.

"I wonder who that can be," said Claud's mother, as she went to open it. "Why, it's Claud!" she cried. And it was. He stood shivering on the doorstep, looking very thin and miserable and cold.

"We're so glad you've come back," said his father. "Sit down and tell us what happened and why you've come back to us."

"I wasn't bad enough," Claud said, and burst into tears. And then, when he had been given something to eat and had warmed himself by the fire, he told his parents about the school and about the very wicked children who were there.

"They were even naughtier than I am," he said. "They turned people into frogs. They turned *me* into a frog until the Witch told them to turn me back. They were much, much naughtier than me. And even though I tried very hard indeed I just couldn't be as bad as the others. And so the Witch said I was too good ever to become a wicked wizard and she sent me away."

"Never mind," said his parents. "We're very pleased to see you. We've missed you."

His brothers and sisters were overjoyed at Claud's return. They laughed when Claud filled their shoes with jam while they were asleep. And they laughed when Claud tied them all to a tree. They even laughed when he pushed them all into the goldfish pond.

"Good old Claud!" they shouted. "We're glad you're back!"

His mother laughed when she

found out he had put beetles into the tea caddy. And his father didn't seem to mind when Claud cut large holes in his newspaper.

"Claud's back and quite his old self again," they said, and smiled at each other.

But soon Claud found that being naughty wasn't as much fun any more. "Nobody seems to mind my tricks," he complained, "even the new ones I learned at the Witch's school. People laugh when I trip them up, or tie their shoelaces together, or put ants in their hair. Why can't they be angry as they used to be?"

So, because being bad wasn't any

38

fun any more, Claud decided to be good instead. Not *completely* good, of course. Every now and again he would throw mud at his brothers and once he even covered the cat with a mixture of shoe polish and marmalade. But people soon forgot that he was once the naughtiest boy in the whole country. And the Chief Witch was so disappointed in Claud that she didn't call again.

The Dragon and the Cockerel

A Story from China

Naomi Adler

There was once a time when dragons were not yet fully formed and when cockerels had tails like those of peacocks and antlers like those of stags. It was during those ancient times that this story occurred.

The celestial emperor ruled over

the sky, the sea and the earth.
Every New Year, he held a great
celebration up in his heavenly
palace in the sky. Important guests
from the many different stars and
planets were invited, among them
the animals of the earth.

The animals of the earth loved
going to this yearly event up in the
sky and they spent many weeks
busily preparing themselves,
making themselves as beautiful as
could be.

Only Dragon was miserable. He
felt himself to be the most dull
and boring creature in all China.
You see, in those days Dragon had
the head of a camel, the eyes of a

demon, the neck and body of a snake, the legs of a tiger and the claws of an eagle. But the fact that he had nothing on top of his head caused him the greatest shame.

One day, as Dragon was swimming in the river, Cockerel came strutting by. Cockerel looked magnificent with his gorgeous tail fanned open and those huge antlers on top of his head. Dragon looked longingly at the antlers.

If only I could have such a splendid headdress, then I wouldn't look so dull any more, he thought to himself.

Suddenly, he had a bright idea. He called out to Cockerel, "Hello

there, Cockerel!"

"Good day, Dragon! Why do you look so sad?" asked Cockerel.

Dragon replied, "I am so sad because I have nothing to wear on my head when I go to the New Year Celebration. Will you lend me your antlers, please, Cockerel?"

Cockerel was amazed. "Certainly

not. I am also invited to the party and I need to wear my antlers myself."

Dragon said, "But Cockerel, you look so beautiful with your gorgeous tail. Your antlers only detract from your splendour."

"No, no, Dragon! I need my antlers," shouted Cockerel.

At that moment a very distinguished carp raised her head out of the water. She had heard the entire conversation and since she was rather fond of Dragon she said, "Dragon is quite right, Cockerel. You are indeed more dazzling without your antlers. They do seem to detract from your splendour. Why don't you lend them to Dragon and I shall guarantee their safe return?"

In the end, vain Cockerel was persuaded that he was even more beautiful without his antlers. Cockerel agreed, "All right, I shall lend you my antlers for one day and one night. You must return them as soon as the New Year celebrations are over."

Dragon promised that he would.

That night at the New Year celebrations everyone admired Dragon. Even the celestial emperor gave him a special welcome, inviting him to sit beside the throne, a place of great honour. Dragon had never experienced such attention and such admiration before. He discovered a new part of himself and he liked it very much. Dragon felt a glow all over his body.

However, Cockerel was extremely jealous when he saw Dragon held in such great esteem and he wished he had kept the antlers for himself. Very early the next morning he rushed over to the river where Dragon lived.

He called out, "Dragon, give me back my antlers!"

Dragon appeared out of the water looking splendid with the huge antlers on top of his head.

He said, "Dear Cockerel, you look so dazzling without the antlers and I look so dull without them, please let me keep them a little longer."

"No!" cried Cockerel. "Give them back at once!"

But Dragon had no intention of keeping his promise. "I must go now," he said. "I have very important matters to attend to at the bottom of the river." And he dived into the water, leaving a furious, screeching Cockerel on the river bank. "Dragon, give me back my antlers! Dragon, give me back my antlers!"

Carp raised her head out of the

water, wondering what all the fuss was about.

"What's the matter, Cockerel?" she asked.

Cockerel replied, "Dragon will not give me back my antlers and it's all your fault, Carp. You guaranteed their safe return."

"I'm sorry, Cockerel. I had no idea that Dragon would become so attached to the antlers. I had no idea that Dragon would look so splendid with the antlers. I had no idea that Dragon would be so transformed by the antlers," said Carp. And she dived back into the deep water, leaving a furious, screeching Cockerel on the river bank, calling out "Cock-a-doodle-doo! Cock-a-doodle-doo!"

So when you next hear a cockerel calling out at dawn, "Cock-a-doodle-doo! Cock-a-doodle-doo!" you will now know that he is calling out, "Dragon, give me back my antlers! Dragon, give me back my antlers!"

As for the dragon, he became China's most revered creature. The celestial emperor bestowed on him the gift of flight, and the guardianship of all the waters in the sky, sea and earth.

The dragon also became the keeper of the magic pearl – but that's another story. Even today, the dragon is invited to celebrate the Chinese New Year and dance the Dance of the Dragon with the people of China.

The Flying Postman

V.H. Drummond

Mr Musgrove was a Postman in a village called Pagnum Moss.

Mr and Mrs Musgrove lived in a house called Fuchsia Cottage. It was called Fuchsia Cottage because it had a fuchsia hedge around it. In the front garden they kept a cow called Nina, and in the back garden they grew strawberries . . . nothing else but strawberries.

Now Mr Musgrove was no ordinary Postman; for instead of walking or trundling about on a bicycle, he flew around in a Helicopter. And instead of pushing letters in through letter boxes, he tossed them into people's windows, singing as he did so: "Wake up! Wake up! For morning is here!"

Thus people were able to read their letters quietly in bed without littering them untidily over the breakfast table.

Sometimes, to amuse the children, Mr Musgrove tied a radio set to the tail of the Helicopter, and flew about in time to the music. He had a special kind of Helicopter that was able to loop the loop and even fly *upside down!*

But one day the Postmaster General and the Postal Authorities sent for Mr Musgrove and said, "It is forbidden to do stunts in the sky. You must keep the Helicopter only for delivering letters and parcels, not for playing about!"

Mr Musgrove felt crestfallen.

After that, Mr Musgrove put his Helicopter away when he had finished work, till one day some of the children came to him and said: "Please do a stunt in the sky for us, Mr Musgrove!"

When he told them he would never do any more stunts, the children felt very sad and some even cried. Mr Musgrove could not bear to see little children sad, so he tied the radio set to the Helicopter, and jumping into the driving seat flew up into the air, to a burst of loud music.

"I'll do just one trick," he said to himself, "a new and very special one!"

The children stopped crying and jumped up and down.

He flew high, high, high up into the sky till he was almost out of sight, then he came whizzing down and swooped low, low, low over the church steeple and away again.

The children, who had scrambled onto a nearby rooftop to get a better view, cried: "It's a lovely trick! Do it again! *Please* do it again!"

So Mr Musgrove flew high, high, high into the sky again and came whizzing and swooping down low, low, low . . . But this time he came *too* low and . . . landed with a whizz! Wang! *Donc!* Right on the church steeple.

The Postmaster General, from his house on the hill, heard the crash and came galloping to the spot on his horse, Black Bertie.

The Postal Authorities also heard the crash, and came running to the spot, on foot.

When he got to the church the Postmaster General dismounted from Black Bertie and, waving his fist at Mr Musgrove, said sternly: "This is a very serious offence! Come down at once!"

"I can't," said Mr Musgrove unhappily. " . . . I'm stuck!"

So the Postal Authorities got a ladder, climbed up the steeple, and lifted Mr Musgrove and the Helicopter down.

When they got to the ground, they examined Mr Musgrove's arms and legs and saw that nothing was broken. They also noticed that the radio set was intact. But the poor Helicopter was seriously damaged; its tail was drooping, its nose was pushed in, and its whole system was badly upset.

"It will take weeks to mend!" said the Postal Authorities.

The Postmaster General turned to Mr Musgrove and said: "For this you will be dismissed from the Postal Service. Hand me your uniform."

Mr Musgrove sadly handed him his peaked hat and his little jacket that had red cord round the edges.

"Mr Boodle will take your place," said the Postmaster General.

Mr Boodle was the Postman from the next village. He did not like the idea of delivering letters for two villages. "Too much for one man on a bicycle," he grumbled, but not loud enough for the Postmaster General to hear.

Mr Musgrove went back to Fuchsia Cottage in his waistcoat.

"I've lost my job, Mrs Musgrove," he said.

Even Nina looked sad and her ears flopped forward.

"Never mind," said Mrs Musgrove, "we will think of a new job for you."

"I am not very good at doing anything except flying a Helicopter and delivering letters," said Mr Musgrove.

So they sat down to think and think, and Nina thought too, with her own special cow-like thoughts.

After a while Mrs Musgrove had a Plan.

"We will pick the strawberries from the back garden and with the cream from Nina's milk we will make some Pink Ice Cream and sell it to people passing by," she cried.

"What a wonderful plan!" shouted Mr Musgrove, dancing happily round. "You *are* clever, Mrs Musgrove!"

Nina looked as if she thought it was a good idea, too, and said "Moo-oo!"

The next day Mr Musgrove went gaily into the back garden and picked a basketful of strawberries. He was careful not to eat any himself, but put them *all* into the

61

basket. Mrs Musgrove milked Nina and skimmed off the cream. And together they made some lovely Pink Ice Cream. Then they put up a notice:

PINK ICE CREAM FOR SALE

Nina looked very proud.

When the children saw the notice they ran eagerly in to buy. And even a few grown-ups came, and said, "Num, Num! What elegant Ice Cream!"

By evening they had sold out, so they turned the board round. Now it said:

PINK ICE CREAM TOMORROW

Every day they made more Pink Ice Cream and every evening they had sold out.

"We are beginning to make quite a lot of lovely money," said Mr Musgrove.

But though they were so successful with their Pink Ice

Cream, Mr Musgrove often thought wistfully of the Helicopter, and his Postman's life. One day as he was exercising Nina in the woods, he met Mr Boodle. Mr Boodle grumbled that he had too much work to do.

"I would rather be a bicycling postman than no postman at all," sighed Mr Musgrove.

Early one morning before the Musgroves had opened their Ice Cream Stall, Nina saw the Postmaster General riding along the road on his horse, Black Bertie. Nina liked Black Bertie, so as they passed she thrust her head through the fuchsia hedge and said, "Moo-oo."

Black Bertie was so surprised that he shied and reared up in the air . . . and tossed the Postmaster General into the fuchsia hedge.

"Moo," said Nina, in alarm, and Mr and Mrs Musgrove came running up.

Carefully they carried him into the house. They laid him on a sofa and put smelling salts under his nose, and tried to make him take some strong, sweet tea, and a little brandy.

But nothing would revive him.

They tried practically everything, including chocolate biscuits and fizzy lemonade, but he

never stirred, till Mrs Musgrove
came towards him carrying a Pink
Ice Cream.

"What's that?" he said, opening
one eye. "It smells good."

So they gave him one.

"It's delicious!" he cried.
"Delicious!"

They gave him another and
another and another . . .

He ate *six!*

"I have recovered now," he said,
standing up, "thanks to your
elegant ice creams, which are the
best I have ever tasted!"

Then he walked outside and
called Black Bertie, who had
walked into the garden and was

eating the grass with Nina. "Come on, Black Bertie, we must go home," he said, and jumped into the saddle and rode away, waving his hand graciously to the Musgroves.

That afternoon, much to the Musgroves' surprise, he reappeared. Nina was careful not to moo through the fuchsia hedge at Black Bertie this time.

"I have reappeared," said the Postmaster General, "because I am so grateful for your kindness and your ice creams that I have prepared a little surprise for you up at my house. Would you like to come and see it, Mr Musgrove?"

"Why, yes!" cried Mr Musgrove, wondering excitedly what on earth it could be.

"Jump on, then!" cried the Postmaster General. "I am afraid there isn't room for Mrs Musgrove too."

At first Mrs Musgrove felt a bit nervous of Black Bertie, but he was too excited to see what the Postmaster General's surprise was really to care.

When they arrived at the Postmaster General's house they put Black Bertie away and gave him a piece of sugar. Then the Postmaster General led Mr Musgrove up the steps of the house into the hall, where stood a large wooden chest. He opened the chest, and drew out . . . Mr Musgrove's peaked cap and little blue jacket with red cord round the edges!

He handed the uniform to Mr Musgrove. "Please wear this," he said, "and become once more the Flying Postman of Pagnum Moss!"

Mr Musgrove was very excited and thanked the Postmaster General three times. Then the Postmaster General took him out into the garden. "Look!" he said, pointing at the lawn, and there stood the Helicopter all beautifully mended!

"Jump in!" cried the Postmaster General. "And be on duty tomorrow morning."

Mr Musgrove raced across the lawn and leapt gleefully in. As he was flying away the Postmaster General called: "Will you sell me six of your beautiful Pink Ice Creams every day, and deliver them to me with the letters every morning?"

"Most certainly!" cried Mr Musgrove, leaning out of the Helicopter and saluting.

"Six Pink Ice Creams . . . I'll keep them in my refrigerator. Two for my lunch, two for my tea and two for my dinner!" shouted the

Postmaster General.

Imagine Mrs Musgrove's and
Nina's surprise when Mr
Musgrove alighted in the front
garden, fully dressed in Postman's
clothes.

"I'm a Postman again!" he cried.
"Oh, happy day!"

"Moo-oo," said Nina, and Mrs
Musgrove clapped her hands.

The next morning he set out to
deliver letters and sing his song:
"Wake up! Wake up! For morning
is here!" and everyone woke up
and shouted: "Mr Musgrove, the
Flying Postman, is back in the sky
again! Hurrah, Hooray!"

Mr Boodle, the grumbling

71

postman, said, "Hurrah, Hooray!"
too, because now he would not
have so much work to do. He was
so excited that he took his hands
off the handlebars, and then he
took his feet of the pedals till the
Postmaster General passed by and,
pointing at him, said, "That is
dangerous and silly."

So he put his hands back on the
handlebars and his feet back on
the pedals.

Mr Musgrove never forgot to
bring the Postmaster General the
six Pink Ice Creams; two for his
lunch, two for his tea and two for
his dinner. And every day clever
Mrs Musgrove made Pink Ice

Cream all by herself, till soon they had enough money to buy a little Helicopter of their very own, which they called Flittermouse. They had Flittermouse made with a hollow in the back for Nina to sit in, and on Saturdays they went to the city to shop, and on Sundays they went for a spin.

Often Mr Musgrove did musical sky stunts in Flittermouse for the children, but he was careful never to fly low over the church steeple.

The Great Sharp Scissors

Philippa Pearce

Once there was a boy called Tim who was often naughty. Then his mother used to say, "*Tim!*" and his father shouted "TIM!" But his granny always said, "Tim's a good boy, really." Tim loved his granny very much. He went to visit her often; and, when he went, his granny always gave him a special present.

One day Tim's mother had a message that his granny was ill. She decided to go to her at once, and Tim said, "I'll come too."

"No, you can't come," said his mother. "Granny's too ill."

Tim scowled and stamped his foot. He was very angry.

"You'll have to stay at home by yourself," said his mother. "You'll have to be good. I won't be long."

Tim said nothing. He just scowled and scowled.

"And if the front door bell rings, Tim, you're not to let any strangers into the house." Then his mother hurried off.

Tim shut the front door, and then he just stood, feeling angrier than he had ever felt before. He listened to his mother's footsteps hurrying down the front path, out through the front gate, and along the street. When he could no longer hear them, he heard other footsteps coming along the street, in at the front gate, and up the front path to the front door. Then the bell rang.

Tim just stood.

The bell rang again.

Still Tim stood.

Then the flap of the letter box went up, and two eyes looked through. A voice – a strange man's voice – called through the letter box: "Tim, aren't you going to let me in?"

Tim decided what to do. He went to the door, and he put the chain on it, and then he opened the door; but the chain prevented its opening wide enough for anyone to get in. Tim peered through the gap of the door, and saw a strange man on the doorstep with a suitcase in his hand.

"I have things here that you might like," said the stranger. He laid his suitcase flat on the doorstep and opened it.

First of all Tim saw a notice inside, and this is what it said:

WE
SELL
KNIVES
SCISSORS
BATTLEAXES

"I'd like a battleaxe," said Tim.

"We're out of battleaxes at the moment," said the stranger.

"Knives?" said Tim.

"Yes," said the stranger. "But what about scissors? I have a most remarkable pair of great sharp scissors." He reached into the suitcase and brought out an enormous pair of scissors. The blades shone sharp and dangerously. "They'll cut anything," said the stranger. "*Anything*."

"I'll have them," said Tim, and he held out his hand.

"Ah," said the stranger, "but you can't have something for nothing. You must pay for these very valuable scissors."

"Wait there," said Tim. He ran and fetched his money box. He reached his hand through the gap of the door and gave the stranger all the money from his money box. In return, the stranger gave Tim the pair of great sharp scissors. Then he smiled at Tim in a way Tim did not like, and went away.

Tim shut the front door and

looked at the scissors in his hand.
He clashed the blades together
and remembered how angry he
was. He decided to try the scissors
out at once. The stranger had said
they would cut anything.
Anything.

He saw his father's coat hanging
in the hall. With his scissors he
cut off all the buttons of his
father's coat. *Snip! Snap! Snip!
Snap!* The buttons all fell to the
floor. It was very easy.

But, of course, even an ordinary
pair of scissors would cut the
buttons off a coat. Tim went into
the living room to find something
more difficult for the great sharp

scissors. He would try them on the carpet.

With his scissors he cut the carpet in two – *snip! snap!* Just like that. Then he cut it again and again and again. He snipped and snapped at the carpet with his great sharp scissors until he had cut it into hundreds of little pieces.

Then Tim tried cutting the wooden leg off a chair. *Snip! Snap!* The great sharp scissors snipped the wooden leg off the chair, just like that. Then Tim snipped the legs off all the chairs and off the table. He cut the sofa in two. *Snip! Snap!*

He tried the great sharp scissors
on the clock on the mantelpiece.
The blades went through the metal
and glass very easily. *Snip! Snap!*
and the clock was in half.

He thought he would cut his
goldfish in its goldfish bowl; but
then he felt sorry for the goldfish.
So he took it out and put it safely

into the handbasin full of water.
Then he did cut the goldfish bowl
with his great sharp scissors. The
blades went through the glass
without even splintering it. *Snip!
Snap!* Just like that. And the
water from the goldfish bowl went
all over the floor.

By now Tim knew that his great
sharp scissors would cut anything.
They would cut through the floors
and the wooden doors. They could
cut through all the bricks of the
walls. They would cut through the
slates of the roof. They would cut
his whole home into a heap of
rubble; and they had begun to do
so.

Tim went and sat on the bottom step of the stairs and cried.

Presently he heard footsteps. They came along the street, in at the front gate, and up the front path to the front door. Then the bell rang.

Tim was very frightened. He was afraid that the same strange man had come back. He sat absolutely still, absolutely quiet.

The bell rang again.

Still Tim sat.

Then the flap of the letter box went up, and two eyes looked through. A voice – a strange woman's voice – called through the letter box: "Tim, aren't you going to open the door a little?"

So Tim opened the door on the chain again, and looked out. On the doorstep stood a strange woman with a lidded basket on her arm. She smiled kindly at Tim, and lifted the lid of her basket.

First of all Tim saw a notice inside, and this is what it said:

> BUY
> GLUES
> INSTANT
> INVISIBLE
> UNBREAKABLE

Tim said: "I've been using a pair of great sharp scissors. I've made an awful, awful mess of everything." He cried again.

The woman said: "I think you need my very best spray-on glue."

"Yes, please," said Tim, and he held out his hand.

"Ah," said the woman, "but you can't have something for nothing, can you?"

Tim said, "I've no money at all. I used it all to buy the scissors."

"I tell you what," said the woman, "you let me have those expensive scissors and I'll let you have my best glue in exchange. You spray the glue round about and it sticks things together instantly, just as they were before."

So Tim gave the woman the great sharp scissors, and she gave him the glue. Then she went off, and he shut the door and took the chain off.

He thought he would try the glue out first on his father's coat. It worked. He sprayed all the buttons back on, as if they had never been cut off.

He went into the living room, and he sprayed all the little pieces of carpet back together again, so that there was one whole carpet again. He sprayed the legs back on to all the chairs and the table. He sprayed the sofa together again. He sprayed the two halves of the clock together again, and at once it began ticking again.

He sprayed the goldfish bowl together again – but, of course, the water was still on the floor. Tim refilled the bowl with water and put the goldfish back.

He'd just got everything straight when he heard the sound of a key in the front-door lock: his mother was home.

His mother walked in, smiling. She said: "Granny's much better, and sends her love." She looked round. "I see you've been a good boy, Tim. Everything's still spick and span."

Tim said: "The goldfish water is

all over the floor."

"Accidents will happen," said his mother. "I'll mop it up." While she mopped it up, she told Tim that his granny had sent him a special present. "She made it for you a long time ago," said Tim's mother. "She told me to take it from her store-cupboard." And Tim's mother brought out from her bag a pot of home-made raspberry jam, which was Tim's favourite jam.

Then Tim's mother made a pot of tea, and she and Tim had tea and new bread and butter and raspberry jam. In the middle of it, Tim's father came home, and he had some of the raspberry jam too.

The Fat Grandmother

Ruth Manning-Sanders

Once upon a time there was a little boy, called Kiriki, who lived underground. He lived with his father and mother, and his sisters and baby brother, and his grandmother. It was a strange place to live, but they had always lived there, and so they didn't think it strange. In front of them was a big lake, and at the back of them rocks went up and up, so smooth and steep that they could not be climbed, and so high that no one had ever seen the top of them. Their house was made of sharkskins, and so was the canoe they went fishing in. The ground was sand and stones, and nothing grew there, so they lived on fish and seaweed, and drank the water that dripped from the high, smooth rocks. They had a dog, and he, too, lived on fish and seaweed. They were all rather thin, except the grandmother who was horribly fat; and they were all happy, except the grandmother, who was selfish and greedy, and always complaining.

As soon as she woke in the morning the grandmother roared out, "Where is my BREAKFAST?" And as soon as she had gobbled up her breakfast, she roared out, "Where is my PIPE?" And as soon as she had smoked her pipe, she roared out, "Where is my DINNER?" And as soon as she had gobbled up her dinner, she roared out, "Are we never going to have anything decent to eat? Where is my SUPPER?" She gobbled and gobbled, and got fatter and fatter, till she was shapeless with fat.

In the lake there lived an old turtle, and Old Turtle and little boy Kiriki were great friends. Old Turtle would poke his flat head out of the water and say, "Coming for a ride?" And then Kiriki would swim out and climb on his back, and off they would go over the glimmering waters of the lake. But however far they went, they never came to the end of the lake. Kiriki thought it had no end; and if Old Turtle knew differently, he never said so.

But one day Old Turtle didn't come and poke his head out of the water. And another day he didn't come, and yet another day. He didn't come for such a long time that Kiriki felt sad.

"I think a shark has eaten Old Turtle," he said to his father.

"Old Turtle has a thick shell and knows how to take care of himself," said his father.

But Kiriki was very sad, for all that.

And then one day Old Turtle came back. He did more than poke his head out of the water, he came right out of the lake and ambled on his funny short legs over the sand and stones to Kiriki. Then he opened his funny thin lips in a kind of smile.

"Where have you been?" said Kiriki.

"Never mind," said Old Turtle.

"I've brought you a present. Put your fingers under my tongue."

Kiriki put his fingers under Old Turtle's tongue.

"Feel anything?" said Old Turtle.

"Only a tiny pebble sort of a thing," said Kiriki.

"Take it out," said Old Turtle.

So Kiriki took the tiny pebble sort of a thing from under Old Turtle's tongue. It was small and dark and hard. Kiriki held it in his hand and looked at it. It didn't seem much of a present.

"It's very precious," said Old Turtle.

"Is it?" said Kiriki.

"I'll tell you what you must do,"

said Old Turtle. "You must plant it."

"Plant it?" said Kiriki. "What's that?"

"At the bottom of the rocks," said Old Turtle.

Kiriki didn't understand a bit, but he liked Old Turtle and was willing to please him. So Old Turtle showed him how to plant the little seed, for that's what it was. He planted it in the sand at the bottom of the high, steep rocks, and mixed rotted seaweed with the sand, as Old Turtle told him to do.

"Now," said Old Turtle, "you must pour water on it night and morning, and watch carefully. And by and by you will see what you will see."

Kiriki did as Old Turtle said. He watched carefully; but the next day he didn't see anything, nor on the day after that, nor on the day after. But, on the fourth morning, when he went to the place with a shell full of water, there sticking up out of the sand, was a thin green spike.

"Something's happened!" shouted Kiriki. "Come and look!"

All the family came running to look, except the grandmother, and she went on gobbling up her breakfast.

What was it? They stared and stared. They had never seen anything like it before.

"What are you all doing over there?" roared the grandmother. "Bring me some MORE BREAKFAST!"

But nobody took any notice of her.

It was a wild vine seed that Kiriki had planted, and the wild vine grew and grew. It shot out leaves, and it shot out branches. It clung to the rocks and it went on growing. It grew as high as his father's head. And then it grew so high that Kiriki had to crane back his head to see the top of it, and then it grew so high that he couldn't see the top of it at all. Its leaves shone and its branches twisted and thickened, and its tendrils clung to the smooth rock like fingers. Kiriki was never tired of watching it.

One day when Kiriki stood

admiring his vine, Old Turtle
came out of the lake and ambled
up to him.

"Well?" said Old Turtle.

"It is indeed a splendid present,"
said Kiriki.

"Then use it, use it!" said Old
Turtle.

"Use it – how?" said Kiriki.

"Climb it, climb it!" said Old
Turtle.

"Shall I?" said Kiriki.

"It's what it's for," said Old
Turtle.

So Kiriki put his feet among the
lowest branches and clung with
his hands to the branches above,
and began to climb.

He climbed and he climbed. He climbed so high that when he looked down he couldn't see his home, and he began to be afraid and thought he had better go back. But he didn't go back, because just then he saw something golden above him, and he thought he must find out what *that* was.

It was a ray of sunlight that Kiriki had seen, but of course he didn't know that. So he went on climbing till he got to the top, and then he stepped out.

He saw blue sky and white clouds, and green grass and flowers, and little woods and great

forests, and rivers flowing, and
hills and valleys, and creatures
moving about. He went up to one
creature and asked its name, and
it said Deer. And he went up to
another and asked its name, and it
said Sheep. And another said Fox,
and another said Hare. And he
went up to a very small creature
and asked *its* name, and it said
Mouse.

"And what place is this?" asked
Kiriki.

"This place?" said Mouse,
scratching his ear. "This place?
Why, it's The Place Where We
Live, of course." And he gave a
twitch of his tail, and darted

under a fallen log.

Kiriki gaped, and Kiriki stared, and then he clapped his hands and jumped for joy. And then he ran and clambered back down the vine as quickly as ever he could.

The family had just finished dinner, and the fat grandmother was sitting on a stone and shouting, "Am I never going to have anything to eat? Where is my SUPPER?"

"And where have you been all this time, Kiriki?" asked his father.

"Oh, oh!" cried Kiriki. "I've been to The Place Where We Live. Come and see! Come and see!"

So the father climbed up the vine

and stepped out. And he was so excited that he came back down the vine like a streak of light.

"Hurry, hurry!" he said. "We're packing up and leaving here! We're going up the ladder to The Place Where We Live."

So they rolled up their sealskin blankets, and each one took a bundle on his back. The father put his stone axe and his fishing lines into his bundle, and the mother put her bone needle and sewing thread made of seal-tendon into her bundle. The father took the dog under his arm, and began to climb; the mother took the baby under her arm, and began to climb; the sisters followed, and Kiriki came last. He stood at the foot of the vine, and Old Turtle stood beside him.

"Come along," said Kiriki to Turtle.

"Come along, indeed!" said Old Turtle. "I can't climb. My legs are the wrong shape."

"Then I'll carry you," said Kiriki.

"I daresay you will," said Old Turtle. "And drop me too – no thank you!"

"But I'm not going without you!" said Kiriki.

"Yes, you are," said Old Turtle. "Now don't cry. Some day I'll swim round."

"Swim round?" said Kiriki. "Can you?"

"Can't I?" said Old Turtle. "But it's a long way, so you mustn't worry if you don't see me for some time."

Then Old Turtle ambled down towards the lake again and Kiriki began to climb up after the others.

The grandmother was sitting on the stone; she was still chewing, and roaring out between the chews, "Where's my SUPPER?"

"Aren't you going?" asked Old Turtle.

The grandmother's mouth was full of grilled salmon.

"I want my SUPPER! Bring me

my SUPPER!" she roared.

"I'm sorry, I can't do that," said Old Turtle, and he ambled into the lake and swam off.

The grandmother went on roaring, "Where's my SUPPER?" and when nobody answered she got off the stone and looked round. And there she was, all alone. So she waddled heavily to the foot of the vine, and roared up, "I want my SUPPER! Who's going to bring me my SUPPER?"

She could see Kiriki far up the vine, and she took hold of the branches and shook them. "Come down!" she roared. "Come down and get my SUPPER!"

But Kiriki only turned his head and shouted, "Come up!" and his voice sounded very small and far away.

The grandmother saw there was no help for it. There was no one left to cook for her or bring her anything. So she put her fat feet on the lower branches, and took hold of the branches above her fat hands, and began to climb. She puffed and groaned and scolded and shouted, but up she went, and up she went, with the branches bending and cracking under her weight.

Kiriki had now got to the top and stepped out with the others, and they were all jumping and shouting for joy in the bright sunlight. And the grandmother climbed on.

"I want my SUPPER! Bring me my SUPPER!" she groaned, for she had no breath left to roar with.

But the higher she went, the slenderer grew the branches, and the more they cracked and bent under her weight. Until the branch that she had her feet on bent right over, and the branch she was clutching with her hands snapped in two, and down, down, *down* she fell.

She knocked herself silly; but by and by she recovered and sat up.

And there was Old Turtle looking at her.

"A pity to be so fat!" said Old Turtle.

"Don't be impertinent!" wheezed the grandmother. "Bring me my SUPPER!"

Old Turtle brought her a

herring, for he was very good-natured.

"Cook it, stupid!" wheezed the grandmother.

"I'm sorry, I can't do that," said Old Turtle. "I don't know how to."

The grandmother threw the herring at him. Old Turtle caught it and put it back in the lake. Then he swam away. The grandmother shouted after him to come back. But he didn't.

Now she was all alone and had to eat seaweed. And the fire had gone out, so she couldn't light her pipe.

She was in a bad way. She ate quantities of seaweed and some cockles and mussels; but she felt sick with all that cold, raw food, and she got thinner and thinner and lighter and lighter, till at last she was just like other people. And when that day came, she thought she would try climbing again.

So she did; and the vine didn't break, and she got to the top and stepped out, and found the family. They had built themselves a fine house of elm bark, and kept a lot of sheep. They had a birch-bark canoe, too, and went fishing in the rivers. They were quite pleased to see the grandmother, but they were busy; they had got out of the way of doing everything she told them, and didn't see why they should begin again. She had to make herself useful, and so she didn't get any fatter than the rest.

Old Turtle was swimming and swimming. And after a long, long time, he came up one of the rivers into The Place Where We Live, and paid Kiriki a visit, as he had promised.

Clem's Dream

Joan Aiken

Clem woke up in his sunny bedroom and cried out, "Oh, I have lost my dream! And it was such a beautiful dream! It sang, and shouted, and glittered, and sparkled – and I've lost it! Somebody pulled it away, out of reach, just as I woke up!"

He looked around – at his bed, his toys, his chair, his open window with the trees outside.

"Somebody must have come in through the window, and they've stolen my dream!"

He asked the Slipper Fairy, "Did you see who stole my dream?"

But the Slipper Fairy had been fast asleep, curled up in his slipper with her head in the toe. She had seen nobody.

He asked the Toothbrush Fairy, "Did you see who stole my dream?"

But the Toothbrush Fairy had been standing on one leg, looking at herself in the bathroom mirror. She had seen nothing.

Clem asked the Bathmat Fairy. He asked the Soap Fairy. He asked

the Curtain Fairy. He asked the
Clock Fairy.

None of them had seen the
person who had stolen his
dream.

He asked the Water Fairy, "Did
you see the person who stole my
dream?"

"Look under your pillow, willow,
willow, willow!" sang the Water
Fairy. "Open your own mouth and
look in, in, in, in! Then, then you'll
know, ho, ho, ho, ho!"

Clem looked under his pillow. He
found a silver coin.

He climbed on a chair, and
looked in the glass, opening his
mouth as wide as it would go.

He saw a hole, where a tooth used to be.

"The Tooth Fairy must have come, while I was asleep. She took my tooth, and paid for it with a silver coin. She must have taken my dream too. But she had no right to do that."

At breakfast, Clem asked, "How can I get my dream back from the Tooth Fairy?"

The Milk Fairy said, "She lives far, far away, on Moon Island, which is the other side of everywhere."

The Bread Fairy said, "She lives in a castle made of teeth, at the top of a high cliff."

117

The Apple Fairy said, "You will have to take her a present. Something round and white. Otherwise she will never give back your dream."

Clem went into the garden. He said, "How can I find my way to Moon Island, on the other side of everywhere? And what present can I take the Tooth Fairy?"

"Go up to the top of the hill, the hill, the hill, the hill," sang the Grass Fairy, "and put your arms round the stone, the stone, the stone that stands there. If your fingers can touch each other, round the other side, then the stone will grant your wish."

118

So Clem ran up to the top of the green, grassy hill.

There stood an old grey stone, tall as a Christmas tree. Clem tried to put his arms round it. But his arms would not quite reach, his fingers would not quite touch.

"You need to grow, to grow, to grow, to grow," sang the Grass Fairy. "Ask my sisters to help you, help you, help you, help you."

So Clem ran back to the house and called for help. The Bread Fairy, the Water Fairy, the Milk Fairy, and the Apple Fairy all came to the top of the hill and helped him. They pulled him

119

longways, they pulled him sideways. By and by, when they had pulled and pulled and pulled, he was able to make his fingers meet round the other side of the old grey stone.

"Now you may have your wish," said the Stone Fairy.

"I wish for a boat," said Clem, "to take me to the Tooth Fairy's castle on Moon Island, on the other side of everywhere."

A laurel leaf fell into the brook, and grew till it was big as a boat. Clem stepped into it.

"Away you go, you go, you go, you go," sang the Water Fairy, and the boat floated away with Clem, down the brook, along the river, and into the wide, wide sea.

The sea is all made of dreams. Looking down, into the deep water, Clem could see many, many dreams. They gleamed and shifted under his boat like leaves made of glass – gold, green, black, and silver. But nowhere could Clem see his own dream, nowhere in all the wide sea.

The boat travelled on, day after day, night after night.

In the distance, Clem saw many monsters. There was the Spinach Monster, all greeny-black, the Shoelace Monster, all tangly, the Stair Monster, all cornery, the

Seaweed Monster, all crackly, and the Sponge Monster, all soggy.

But the Water Fairy tossed handfuls of water at them, and they did not dare come too near.

At last the boat came to Moon Island, on the other side of everywhere. Moon Island is round as a wheel. Its rocky beaches are covered with oysters, and black stones as big as apples. Up above are high white cliffs. And on top of the highest cliff of all stands the Tooth Fairy's castle, which is all made out of teeth.

"How shall I ever manage to climb up that cliff?" said Clem. "And what present can I take the

Tooth Fairy, so that she will give
me back my dream?"

"Sing a song to the oysters on
the beach," the Water Fairy told
him. "They are very fond of
songs."

So Clem sang:

"*Night sky*
Drifting by
How can I climb the rock so
high?
Moon beam
Star gleam
Where shall I find my stolen
dream?"

All the oysters on the beach sighed with pleasure, and opened their shells to listen to Clem's song.

The King of the Oysters said, "Stoop down, Clem, feel with your finger inside my shell, and you will find a pearl. Take it to the Tooth Fairy, and perhaps she will give you back your dream."

Clem stooped and gently poked his finger inside the big oyster shell. There he found a pearl as big as a plum. It just fitted in the palm of his hand. He also picked up one of the round black stones off the beach.

"Thank you!" he said to the King of the Oysters. "That was kind of you. I will take this beautiful pearl to the Tooth Fairy, and perhaps she will give me back my dream. But how shall I ever climb up this high cliff?"

"Sing your song again, again, again," sang the Water Fairy. "And perhaps somebody else will help you."

So Clem sang:

"Night, sleep,
Ocean deep,
How shall I climb the cliff so
steep?
Rain, mist
Snow, frost
How shall I find my dream
that's lost?"

Then snowflakes came pattering down out of the sky and built Clem a staircase of white steps that led, back and forth, back and forth, criss-cross, all the way up the high cliff.

And so Clem was able to climb up, step by step, step by step, until he came to the very top, where the Tooth Fairy's castle was perched.

The door was made of driftwood, white as paper.

Clem knocked on the door with his black stone. When he shook the stone, it rattled, as if it had loose teeth inside it.

Clem knocked once. He knocked twice. He knocked three times.

"Who is banging on my door?" cried an angry voice.

"It's me, Clem! I have come to ask for my dream!"

Slowly the door opened, and the Tooth Fairy looked out.

The Tooth Fairy is the oldest fairy in the world. Before the last dragon turned to stone, she was building her castle, and she will be building it when the seeds from the last thistle fly off into space. Her eyes are like balls of snow, and her hands are like bunches of thorns. Her feet are like roots. Her teeth are like icicles.

"Who are you?" said the Tooth Fairy. "How dare you come knocking at my door? I never give back a tooth. Never!"

"I'm Clem. And I don't want my tooth back. I want my dream back!"

The Tooth Fairy gave Clem a crafty look.

"How can you be certain that I

have your dream?"

"I'm certain," said Clem.

"And if I have it, here in my castle, how can you find it?"

"I'll know it when I see it," said Clem.

"Oh, very well. You may come in and look for it. But you may stay only seven minutes."

So Clem went into the Tooth Fairy's castle – along wide halls and into huge rooms.

The fairy shut the door behind him, and pulled the bolt, which was made from a serpent's tooth.

Clem wandered all over the castle – up winding stairways, round corners, through galleries, up onto the tops of towers, out on balconies, down into cellars, under arches, across courtyards.

Everything was white, and there was not a single sound to be heard. Not a mouse, not a bird.

He began to fear that he would never find his dream.

"You have had six minutes!" called the Tooth Fairy.

Her voice rang like a bell in the hollow castle.

But then, just after that, Clem heard the tiniest tinkle, like water dripping into a pool.

"Look up," whispered the Water Fairy. "Look up, up, up, up!"

Clem looked up, into a round,

empty tower. And high, high, high, high, far, far up, he saw something flutter – something that gleamed, and twinkled, and shone, and sparkled.

"It's my dream!" shouted Clem joyfully. "Oh, oh, oh, it's my beautiful, beautiful dream!"

At the sound of his voice, the dream came floating and fluttering down from the high cranny where the Tooth Fairy had hidden it; like a falling leaf it came floating and fluttering down, and then wrapped itself lovingly all round Clem.

"This is my own dream," he told the Tooth Fairy. "And here is a pearl, which I brought for you.

Now I shall take my dream home."

At the sight of Clem, joyfully hugging his dream, the Tooth Fairy became so sad that she began to melt. She grew smaller, like a lump of ice in the sun.

"Don't, don't, don't take your dream away, Clem! Please, please leave it with me!" she begged. "It is the only beautiful thing I have, in all this silent whiteness. It is the most beautiful thing I have ever seen. If you leave it with me I will give you a hundred years!"

"I don't want a hundred years," said Clem. "I would rather have my dream."

"I will give you a carriage, to

travel faster than the sun!"

"I would rather have my dream."

"I will give you a bonfire that you can carry in your pocket."

"I would rather have my dream."

"I will give you a ray of light that can cut through stone."

"I would rather have my dream."

"I will give you a garden that grows upside down and backwards."

"I would rather have my dream."

"I will give you a word that will last for ever."

"I would rather have my dream."

When the Tooth Fairy saw that Clem really meant to take his dream away, she grew sadder still.

"Very well," she said at last. "Give me the pearl, then."

She sighed, such a long deep sigh that the whole castle trembled. Then she pulled back the bolt, made from a serpent's tooth, and opened the door. Clem walked out of the castle.

When he turned to wave goodbye to the Tooth Fairy, she was sitting huddled up on a tooth. She looked so old and small and withered and pitiful that he began to feel sorry for her. He stood thinking.

"Listen!" he called after a minute or two. "Would you like to *borrow* my dream? Suppose you keep it until the next time you come to take one of my teeth. How about that?"

"Yes! *Yes!* YES!"

Her white eyes suddenly shone like lamps.

So Clem gently let go of his dream and it fluttered away, back into the Tooth Fairy's castle.

"Goodbye, Dream – for a little while!" he called. "I'll see you next Tooth-day."

"Wait!" called the Tooth Fairy. "Since you have been so kind, Clem, I'll give you back your pearl."

"No, no, keep it, keep it! Why would I want a pearl? Put it into the wall of your castle."

Clem ran down the stair that had built itself of snow. On the stony beach down below, his boat was waiting for him. He jumped into it, and it raced back over the sea, over the floating dreams, red, black, silver and green like leaves.

But Clem looked behind him and saw his own dream waving and fluttering like a flag from the tower of the Tooth Fairy's castle, and the pearl shining like a round eye in the wall.

"It won't be many months before she comes with the dream," thought Clem, and he poked with his finger in the gap between his teeth, where already he could feel a new tooth beginning to grow.

When he arrived home the Bread Fairy, the Milk Fairy, and the Apple Fairy were there to welcome him.

"I have lent my dream to the Tooth Fairy," he told them. "But it won't be many months before she brings it back."

And he ran upstairs, washed his face, brushed his teeth, and jumped into bed.

He took with him the round black stone, which rattled gently when he shook it.

"The Tooth Fairy will look after my dream," he told the Slipper Fairy and the Clock Fairy.

"She has it safe." Then he fell asleep.

When Clem was fast asleep, still holding the black stone, which rattled gently to itself, all the fairies came to look at him.

"He doesn't know," said the Water Fairy, "he doesn't know that he has brought away the most precious thing of all, all, all, all, all."

"If he ever learns how to open up that stone," said the Bread Fairy, "he will be more powerful than any of us."

"He will be able to grow apple trees on the moon," said the Apple Fairy.

"Or grass on Mars," said the Grass Fairy.

"Or make the tick-tock Time turn backwards," ticked the Clock Fairy.

"Well, let us hope that he uses it sensibly, sensibly, sensibly," said the Soap Fairy softly.

"Let us hope so," said the Curtain Fairy.

"Let us hope so," said the Bathmat Fairy.

But Clem slept on, smiling, holding the black stone tightly in his hand.

And, by and by, he began to dream again.

The Hobyahs

Andrew Matthews

On the west side of Waffam lay Shivery Wood. Near Shivery Wood stood a thatched cottage, and in that cottage Mr and Mrs Trotter lived with their little dog, Turpin.

Every night when the clock struck twelve, the Hobyahs would come out of the wood on tiptoe, rolling their eyes, and licking their lips, and clicking their claws, whispering:

*"We'll break down the door
with a bash and a crack!
We'll carry the Trotters
away in a sack!"*

But every night Turpin heard
the Hobyahs coming, and he
barked so loudly that he
frightened them away.

Mr and Mrs Trotter knew
nothing about the Hobyahs, but
they knew Turpin was barking
because it woke them up.

"If that dog of ours doesn't stop
barking in the middle of the
night," said Mr Trotter, "I shall
have to take off his legs."

That night, just after the clock struck twelve, the Hobyahs came out of the wood on tiptoe, rolling their eyes, and licking their lips, and clicking their claws, and whispering:

"We'll break down the door
with a bash and a crack!
We'll carry the Trotters
away in a sack!"

As soon as Turpin heard the Hobyahs, he barked as loudly as he could and frightened them away. But Mr Trotter woke up and got out of bed and he took off Turpin's legs.

"And if that doesn't do the trick,

I'll have to unscrew your head!"
said Mr Trotter.

Well, the next night, just after
the clock struck twelve, the
Hobyahs came out of the wood on
tiptoe, rolling their eyes, and
licking their lips, and clicking
their claws, and whispering:

> *"We'll break down the door*
> *with a bash and a crack!*
> *We'll carry the Trotters*
> *away in a sack!"*

Turpin heard the Hobyahs and
he barked loudly to frighten them
away, but he woke up his master.
Mr Trotter got out of bed and he
unscrewed Turpin's head.

"That'll fix you and your barking once and for all!" he said.

Well, the next night, just after midnight, the Hobyahs came out of the wood on tiptoe, rolling their eyes, and licking their lips, and clicking their claws and whispering:

"We'll break down the door
with a bash and a crack!
We'll carry the Trotters
away in a sack!"

This time, there was no barking from Turpin to see them off, so the Hobyahs broke down the door of the cottage with a bash and a crack, and they popped Mrs

Trotter into a sack, and they carried her back to their cave in the forest, and they hung the sack from a nail in the wall.

They didn't catch Mr Trotter, because he hid himself under the bed. As soon as he was sure the Hobyahs had gone, Mr Trotter came out of hiding.

"I've been so stupid!" he said. "Turpin was keeping the Hobyahs away, and I went and took off his legs, and unscrewed his head. Now the Hobyahs have taken away my wife and I don't know what I shall do!"

Mr Trotter went to find Turpin and he stuck his legs back on and screwed his head back. Turpin started sniffing the ground, and when he smelled the Hobyahs, he growled.

Off he went into Shivery Wood, following the scent, with Mr Trotter close behind him. When they reached the Hobyahs' cave

the Hobyahs were out digging turnips.

Turpin's clever nose soon found Mrs Trotter in the sack.

As soon as she was free, Mrs Trotter gave her husband a hug and said, "Back home as fast as we can! The Hobyahs will be here any minute!"

Mr and Mrs Trotter hurried home, but Turpin hopped into the sack and waited. Before long, he heard the Hobyahs' tippy toes, and roly eyes, and licky lips, and clicky claws, and their voices whispering:

"Ha, ha, ha, ha!

Hee, hee, hee, hee!
We'll have Mrs Trotter
with turnips for tea!"

When the Hobyahs were all in the cave, Turpin jumped out of the sack, snarling and barking and biting.

And the Hobyahs ran. They ran out of the wood, through the village, over the top of Lumpy Tump and all the way to the seashore. Then they dived into the sea and swam down to the bottom, and there they stayed.

And that's why there are no Hobyahs in Shivery Wood nowadays.

The Manatee

Philippa Pearce

The first time that Totty slept away from home was when he went to stay with his grandfather for one night. He went with his eldest sister; they slept in two separate beds in the same bedroom. That night Totty didn't feel at all homesick. After all, he had his sister.

Then Totty went all by himself to spend a night with his

grandfather. He had said he wanted to do that.

On that visit, in the afternoon, Totty and his grandfather went to the park together, and Totty's grandfather pushed him high on the swings. Then they came home and had tea with baked beans and ice cream afterwards.

After tea, Totty's grandfather got out a book of wild animal pictures to show him. Totty's best animals were fierce lions and tigers and jaguars and ravening wolves. Almost at the end of the book there was a picture of two dark grey creatures lolling in the shallow water of some strange river. They had heavy heads and tiny eyes and huge, bristling upper lips. Their forelegs looked rather like canoe-paddles, and Totty couldn't see any back legs at all.

"They're fish," said Totty.

"No," said his grandfather. "They're not fish. They're animals called Manatees. It says so here."

Totty stared at the Manatees in the picture, and thought. Then he asked: "What do Manatees eat?"

But either his grandfather did not want to answer that question, or he did not hear it – he was an old man, and rather deaf. He shut the animal book with a snap and said: "Time for bed, young Totty!"

So Totty went to bed.

He slept in the same bedroom as before; but, of course, the other bed in it was empty this time. All the same, it had been properly made up with a pillow and sheets and blankets. This was in case Totty's sister had come, too.

Totty's grandfather said goodnight to Totty and turned off the bedroom light. He left the bedroom door a little ajar, so that Totty could see the light on the landing outside.

Totty heard his grandfather go downstairs, and then he heard the sound of television. His grandfather would probably watch television all evening.

Totty did not go to sleep. He didn't feel lonely; but, all the same, he thought it would have been nice to have someone sleeping in the other bed. After a while, he got up and went out onto the landing, where it was light. He looked

down the stairs. The stairs were painted white, with a narrow brown carpet coming up the middle of them. Totty wasn't used to stairs: his family lived in a flat.

After a while he went back into his bedroom, closing the door again so that it was a little ajar, as before. When he had opened the door to go onto the landing, and now when he almost closed it, the hinges had creaked. Totty's grandfather had already said they needed a spot of oil. He had said this was a little job that Totty and he could do tomorrow morning.

Totty got back into bed, and this time he began to go to sleep.

Suddenly he was wide awake again because his grandfather had turned off the television set. Now he could hear his grandfather locking up the house, getting ready to go to bed. His grandfather turned out all the lights. He went to bed.

Now there was no light from the landing, shining through the narrow opening of Totty's door. Everything was dark.

Totty lay awake. He couldn't see anything; but after a while, he thought he had heard something. He thought he heard a tiny, soft little sound like a *flop* on the stairs – far down, at the bottom of the stairs.

156

Had he heard it, or hadn't he?

There was no one but himself and his grandfather in the house, so there just couldn't be a person creeping up the stairs.

All the same, he became almost sure that there was someone or something at the bottom of his grandfather's stairs, just beginning to climb them.

He held his breath so that he could listen as carefully as possible, and he shut his eyes, too. As soon as he shut his eyes, he saw quite clearly what it was at the bottom of the stairs, preparing to come up them. It was a Manatee.

The Manatee had lifted its

bristly face and was looking with its beady eyes towards the landing upstairs. It had put one of its forelegs on the bottom step of the stairs, and now – a heave of its great, grey weight and it was up the first step.

Totty opened his eyes, and then he couldn't see the Manatee on the stairs any more. He could only see the darkness. He couldn't hear the Manatee, either, but that was because he had to breathe and his heart had to beat; and the sound of his own breathing and the beating of his own heart covered the very slight, soft sound that even the most cunning Manatee would have to make as it came upstairs.

Totty said to himself: "If I yell and yell, Grandfather will wake up and hear me and come. I'll tell him there's a Manatee on the stairs, and he'll go and look, and say there's nothing there. Then he'll go back to bed, and I shall lie here in the dark again, all by myself, and the Manatee will start coming up the stairs all over again."

So Totty didn't call to his grandfather – yet.

He didn't make any noise at all that might stop his hearing the Manatee coming up the stairs. He breathed as quietly as he could, and he didn't move any part of his body, to make even the smallest rustle of the sheets.

The Manatee must be reaching the top of the stairs by now.

Totty tried to lie still and silent as a stone.

Now the Manatee would be snuffling round the landing. It found Totty's bedroom door ajar. It didn't find his door by accident: the Manatee was looking for it. It had known that Totty's door would be ajar.

Now, Totty thought, *if the Manatee pushes the door wider open to come in, the hinges will creak. If the hinges creak, the Manatee is coming in.*

160

But the Manatee did not push the door wider open. Instead, it began to make itself thin. Totty knew why the Manatee was making itself thin. It made itself thinner and thinner, until at last it was thin enough to slide through the crack of the door into Totty's bedroom.

Now, thought Totty, *the Manatee is going to rear up at the foot of the bed. The Manatee is a man-eater. It wants to eat* me. *So yell – yell – YELL –*

Totty tried to open his mouth to yell for his grandfather, but his mouth wouldn't open. His teeth, clamped together, kept it shut. In vain he struggled and struggled to open his mouth and yell. As he tried, he thought desperately, *Suppose I could* persuade *the Manatee not to eat me? Suppose I could persuade it that there was something else that it would be nicer to do?*

Totty was thinking hard, and he thought one thing, and the Manatee waiting at the foot of his bed listened to Totty's thought. It paid attention. The Manatee began to heave itself slowly, slowly across the bedroom floor from Totty's bed to the other bed, that was empty. Slowly, slowly – with Totty thinking hard all the time –

the Manatee heaved itself up onto the bed. Very carefully indeed, so as not to disturb the bedclothes by a rumple or even a wrinkle, it slipped into the bed between the sheets.

Inside his head Totty heard the Manatee say "Ah!" in a deep, bristly voice. Then it said: "How beautifully comfortable!" Then it fell fast asleep.

Totty waited a little while until he was sure the Manatee was asleep. Then he went to sleep, too.

He felt quite safe.

When Totty woke in the morning, the Manatee had gone. In going, it had not marked the cleanness of the sheets on the other bed nor disturbed its smoothness.

Totty went down to breakfast with his grandfather. He asked him a question about Manatees. His grandfather fetched the book of animal pictures, and found the right page. He read what the book said about Manatees.

" 'They are slow in their movements'," read Grandfather.

"Yes," said Totty.

" 'And perfectly harmless'."

"Not man-eating?" said Totty.

"No. It says here that they are vegetarian. They eat only water weeds. They live in water."

"They never come right out onto dry land and into houses?"

"Never."

Totty was disappointed. He would have liked to have spent another night in his grandfather's house, with the Manatee sleeping in the bed next to his. It would have been a friendly, comfortable thing to do.

But you couldn't expect a water animal to heave itself up a staircase and into a bed, night after night, even to please a friend. Totty knew that. Once would have to be enough.

The Musicians
of Bremen

The Brothers Grimm

Once there was a donkey who worked very hard for his master. But when he became old and tired, he could no longer carry such large loads, and it became clear that his master would not keep him for much longer.

The best thing for me to do, thought the donkey, *would be to*

*take myself off before that day
comes. I shall go to Bremen and
become a musician. My braying has
often been noticed.*

So early one morning, the
donkey set off for Bremen. On the
way, he met a dog, sheltering by a
tumbledown wall.

"You look rather sorry for yourself, old friend," said the donkey.

"I am too old to go hunting with
my master," growled the dog.
"Now, he hardly feeds me at all."

"Come with me to Bremen!"
laughed the donkey.

"If I bray and you bark, we shall
make fine music!"

Off went the donkey and the dog.

Before long, they met a cat, crouched on a roof.

"It's a fine morning!" called the donkey.

But the cat meowed pitifully.

"Maybe it is for you," she called, "but I am old and even the mice laugh at me."

"Come with us and be a musician!" called the donkey and the dog.

"Your voice is still strong and tuneful."

So the donkey and the dog and the cat went on their way to Bremen, singing as they went.

Now the musicians were making a very loud noise, but as they passed a farmer's barn, they heard a noise that was so loud it drowned even their strange and wonderful singing.

"Cock-a-doodle-doo! Cock-a-doodle-doo!"

"Goodness me," said the donkey. "This is a strange time of day for a rooster to be crowing."

"What else can I do?" called the rooster. "The farmer is having some friends to dinner tonight. I'm very much afraid that I'm the main course!"

"Don't worry," the donkey replied. "I can think of a much better use for your voice. You just come along with us."

And so the donkey and the dog and the cat and the rooster went on towards Bremen.

By the evening, the animals were tired. They needed a warm place to sleep and a fine dinner to end the day. At last, in the distance, they saw the lighted window of a little cottage.

When they reached it, the rooster flew up and looked in the window.

"I can see four robbers, sitting down to a delicious meal!" he called.

"That sounds just right for us," said the donkey. "And what is more, I have a plan."

So the dog climbed on the donkey's back. And the cat climbed on the dog's back. And the rooster perched on the cat's back. Then the animals went right up to the window and sang their music at the tops of their voices. It was an extraordinary sound!

"It's a ghost!" cried one robber, and rushed from the room.

"It's a goblin!" cried another, scrambling after him as fast as he could.

"It's a troll!" called the third, stumbling over his chair.

"I want my mother!" sobbed the last robber. "Wait for me!"

In just a few minutes, the four

animal friends had taken the robbers' places at the table and were enjoying a delicious meal.

Later that night, the animals slept soundly in the warm, comfortable cottage. But the robbers had talked themselves out of their fear and crept back to see if the coast was clear. Luckily, the dog's sharp ears heard them coming, so the animals hid behind the door and waited silently in the darkness.

As soon as the robbers were inside the cottage, the donkey cried, "Now!" and took hold of one robber's trousers with his strong yellow teeth. In a flash, the

dog had fastened his jaws around
the second robber's ankles. The
cat had jumped and sunk her
claws into the third robber's
shoulder. And the rooster had
pecked the nose of the fourth
robber so hard that it was never
the same again.

Well, those robbers ran away even faster than they had the first time, leaving the four friends in peace. The cottage was so charming that they never did reach Bremen, but they made time for their singing practice every day. And if you had ever heard them, you would know that the good people of Bremen had a very lucky escape indeed!

The Man Whose Mother was a Pirate

Margaret Mahy

There was once a little man who had never seen the sea, although his mother was an old pirate woman. The two of them lived in a great city, far, far from the seashore.

The little man had a brown suit with black buttons, and a brown tie and shiny shoes – all most respectable and handsome. He worked in a neat office and wrote down rows of figures in books, and ruled lines under them. And before he spoke, he always coughed "*Hrrrrrm!*"

Well, one day his mother said, "Shipmate, I want to see the sea again. I want to get the city smoke out of my lungs and put the sea salt there instead. I want to fire my old silver pistol off again, and see the waves jump with surprise."

"*Hrrrrm*, Mother," the little man said, very respectful and polite. "I haven't got a car or even a horse, and no money to get one or the other. All we have is a wheelbarrow and a kite."

"We must make do," his mother answered sharply. "I will go and load my silver pistol and polish my cutlass."

The little man went to work. He asked Mr Fat (who was the man he worked for), "*Hrrrrm*, Mr Fat! May I have two weeks to take my mother to the seaside?"

"I don't go to the seaside," Mr Fat snapped out. "Why should you need to go?"

"*Hrrrrm*, it is for my mother," the little man explained.

"I don't see why you should want to go to the seaside," said Mr Fat crossly. "There is nothing there but water . . . salty at that! I once found a penny in the sand, but that is all the money I have ever made at the seaside. There is nothing financial about the sea."

"*Hrrrrm*, it is for my mother," the little man said again. "I will be back in two weeks."

"Make sure you are!" Mr Fat answered crossly.

So they set off, the little man pushing his mother in the wheelbarrow, and his mother holding the kite.

His mother's short grey hair ruffled merrily out under the green scarf she wore tied around her head. Her gold earrings challenged the sun, throwing his own light back to him. Between her lips was her old black pipe, and she wore, behind her ear, a rose that matched her scarlet shawl. The little man wore his brown suit and boots, all buttoned and tied. He trotted along pushing the wheelbarrow.

As they went, his mother talked about the sea. She told him of its voices:

"It sings at night with a sad booming voice. Under the sun it laughs and slaps the side of the ship in time to its laughter. Yes, and then, when a storm comes, it screams and hates poor sailors.

And the sea is a great gossip! What is the weather at Tierra del Fuego? Is the ice moving in Hudson Bay? Where are the great whales sailing? The sea knows it all, and one wave mutters and whispers it to another, and to those who know how to listen."

"*Hrrrrm*, yes indeed, Mother," the little man said, pattering the wheelbarrow along. His shoes hurt rather.

"Where are you going?" a farming fellow asked him.

"*Hrrrrm*, I'm taking Mother to the seaside," the little man answered.

"I wouldn't go there," the

181

farming fellow remarked. "It's not a safe place at all. It's wet and cold and gritty, I'm told . . . not comfortable like a cowshed."

"*Hrrrrm*, it's very musical, Mother says," the little man replied.

In his mind he heard the laughter and the boom and the

scream and the song of the sea. He trotted along, pushing the wheelbarrow. His mother rested her chin on her knees as she jolted along.

"Yes, it is blue in the sunshine," she said. "And when the sun goes in, the sea becomes green. Yet in the twilight I have seen it grey and serene, and at night, inky-black and wild, it tosses beside the ship. Sunrise turns it to burning gold, the moon to liquid silver. There is always change in the sea."

They came to a river . . . There was no boat. The little man tied the wheelbarrow with his mother in it, to the kite string. His neat little moustache was wild and ruffled by the wind. Now he ran barefoot.

"*Hrrrrm!* Hold on tight, Mother," he called.

Up in the air they went as the wind took the kite with it. The little man dangled from the kite string and his mother swung in her wheelbarrow basket.

"This is all very well, Sam," she shouted to him, "but the sea – ah the sea! It rocks you to sleep, tosses you in the air, pulls you down to the deep. It speeds you along and holds you still. It storms you and calms you. The sea is bewitching but bewildering."

184

"*Hrrrrm*, yes, Mother," the little man said. As he dangled from the kite string he saw the sea in his mind – the blue and the green of it, the rise and the fall, the white wings of the birds, the white wings of the ships.

The kite let them down gently on the other side of the river.

"Where are you going?" asked a philosopher fellow who sat there.

"*Hrrrrm!* I'm taking Mother to the sea," the little man told him.

"Why do you want to go there?"

"*Hrrrrm!* The sea is something very special," the little man answered him. "It is full of music and strange songs and stories, full

185

of shadows and movement. My mother is very fond of it."

"You love it too, don't you, little man?" said the philosopher.

"Well," the little man replied, "the more I hear my mother talk about it, the more the thought of it swells inside me, all glowing and wonderful."

Then the philosopher shook his head. "Go back, go back, little man," he cried, "because the wonderful things are always less wonderful than you hope they will be . . . The sea is less warm, the joke less funny, the taste is not as good as the smell."

The old pirate mother called

from the wheelbarrow, waving her cutlass.

"I must go," the little man said shyly.

Off he ran, and as he trundled his mother away, he noticed that two buttons had popped off his coat.

Something new came into the wind scent.

"Ah, there's the salt!" His mother sniffed the wind. "There's nothing as joyful as a salt sea wind."

Suddenly they came over a hill . . . Suddenly there was the sea.

The little man could only stare. He hadn't dreamed of the BIGNESS of it, of the blueness of it. He hadn't thought it would roll like kettledrums, and swish itself onto the beach. He heard the strange, wild music of waves and seabirds, and smelled wet sand and seaweed and fish and ropes and driftwood. The little man opened his eyes and his mouth, and the drift and the dream of it, the weave and the wave of it, the fume and the foam of it flooded into him and never left him again. At his feet the sea stroked the sand with soft little paws. Farther out the waves pounced and bounced like puppies. And out beyond, again and again, the great, graceful breakers moved like kings into court, trailing the sea like a peacock-patterned robe behind them.

Then, with joy, the little man and his mother danced hornpipes along the beach. How the little man's neat clothes grew wild and happy to be free.

A rosy sea captain came along. "Well, here are two likely people," the captain said. "Will you be my bosun, madam? And you, little man, can be the cabin boy."

"*Hrrrrm*, thank you!" said the little man.

"Say 'Aye, aye, sir!'" roared the captain.

"Aye, aye, sir!" smartly replied

189

the little man as if he had never had a "*Hrrrrm!*" in his throat. And then he sang as he twirled on his toes:

> "*No wonder that*
> *I dance on my toes.*
> *Goodbye Mr Fat*
> *And figures in rows,*
> *Figures in rows*
> *And ink's blue gleaming.*
> *For where the sea goes*
> *Is beyond all dreaming.*"

So Sailor Sam went onto the ship with his pirate mother and the sea captain, and a year later somebody brought Mr Fat a letter that had been washed ashore in a bottle.

"Having a wonderful time," it read. "Why don't *you* run off to sea, too?"

And if you want any more moral to this story, you must go to sea and find it.

The Little Boy's Secret

David L. Harrison

One day a little boy left
school early because he had
a secret to tell his mother. He was
in a hurry to get home, so he took
a short cut through some woods
where three terrible giants lived.
He hadn't gone far before he met
one of them standing in the path.

When the giant saw the little
boy, he put his hands on his hips
and roared, "What are you doing

here, boy? Don't you know whose woods these are?"

"I'm on my way home," answered the little boy. "I have a secret to tell my mother."

That made the giant furious. "Secret?" he bellowed. "What secret?"

"I can't tell you," said the little boy, "or it wouldn't be a secret any more."

"Then I'm taking you to our castle!" said the giant. Stooping down, he picked up the little boy and popped him into his shirt pocket.

Before long the first giant met a second giant who was twice as big, three times as ugly, and four times as fierce.

"What's that in your pocket?" he asked the first giant.

"A boy," he answered. "Says he has a secret that he won't tell us."

When the second giant heard that, he laughed a wicked laugh. "Won't tell us, eh?" he chuckled. "Well, we'll just see about that! To the castle with him!"

The giants thumped on down the path. In a short time they came to a huge stone castle beside a muddy river.

At the door they met the third giant, who was five times bigger, six times uglier, and seven times fiercer than the second giant.

"What's that in your pocket?" he asked the first giant.

"A boy," he answered.

"A boy!" chuckled the third giant. He brought his huge eye close to the pocket and peered in.

"Says he has a secret he won't tell us," said the first giant.

When the third giant heard that, he laughed a terrible laugh. "Won't tell us, eh?" he asked. "Well, we'll just see about that! On the table with him!"

The first giant took the little boy from his pocket and set him on the kitchen table. Then all three giants gathered round and peered down at him.

The little boy looked at the first giant. He looked at the second giant. He looked at the third giant.

They were truly enormous and dreadful to behold.

"Well?" said the first giant.

"We're waiting," said the second giant.

"I'll count to three," said the third giant.

"One . . . two . . ."

The little boy sighed a big sigh.

"Oh, all right," he said. "I suppose I can tell you. But if I do, you must promise to let me go."

"We promise," answered the giants. But they all winked sly winks at one another and crossed their fingers behind their backs because they didn't really mean to let him go at all.

The little boy turned to the first giant. "Bend down," he said. The giant leaned down and the little boy whispered into his ear.

When the giant heard the secret, he leaped up from the table. His knees shook. His tongue hung out. "Oh, no!" he shouted. "That's terrible!" And he dashed from the castle, ran deep into the woods, and climbed to the top of a tall tree. He didn't come down for three days.

The second giant scowled at the little boy.

"What's wrong with him?" he asked.

"Never mind," said the little boy. "Just bend down."

The giant leaned down and the little boy stood on tiptoe and whispered into his ear.

When the giant heard the secret, he leaped up so fast that he knocked his chair over. His eyes rolled. His ears twitched. "Let me get away," he roared. And he raced from the castle, ran over the hills and crawled into the deepest, darkest cave he could find.

The third giant frowned down at the little boy.

"What's wrong with them?" he asked.

"Never mind," said the little boy. "Just bend down."

The giant leaned down and the little boy climbed onto a teacup and whispered into his ear.

When the giant heard the secret, he jumped up so fast that he ripped the seat of his trousers. His teeth chattered. His hair stood on end. "Help!" he cried. "Help!" And he dashed from the castle and dived head first into the muddy river.

The castle door had been left open, and since the giants had promised the little boy that he could go, he walked out and went home.

At last he was able to tell his mother his secret; but she didn't yell and run away. She just put him to bed and gave him some supper.

The next morning when the little

boy woke up, he was covered from head to toe with bright red spots.

"Now I can tell *everybody* what my secret was," he said with a smile. "My secret was . . . *I'm getting the measles!*"

The Hare and the Spoilt Queen

Lynne Reid Banks

Once there was a spoilt queen. She was bad-tempered and terribly unfair. She blamed her people for everything that went wrong.

For instance, at her coronation, just as the Archbishop set the crown on her head, she bent over to scratch a sudden itch on her instep and her crown fell off and rolled down the steps leading to the throne.

She ranted and raved that it was everyone's fault but hers, and spoilt the whole occasion so thoroughly that nobody took pictures of her. Then she got furious again because her picture wasn't in the papers or on television. She closed all the TV stations and newspapers down, so nobody knew what was happening.

To cheer her up, her people held a big festival for her. They planned it weeks in advance and worked very hard to make it a success. When the day came – it rained.

The queen jumped up and down, shouting that it was all their fault for choosing a rainy day to hold the festival on.

All the people felt very miserable. The queen wasn't speaking to anyone. There was no telly. Nobody knew what to do.

One day the spoilt queen was out walking in the palace garden with two scared ladies-in-waiting. They kept just behind her and held hands because they were so frightened that she would find something to blame them for.

She pulled an apple crossly off a tree and bit into it. Then she spat out the piece, turned on the two ladies-in-waiting and screamed:

"This apple is *sour*! How dare you let me pick it when it's not ripe!"

And she threw it straight at them.

They didn't bother arguing that it wasn't their fault. They just turned and ran.

That left the queen on her own. She stamped and fumed in the long grass, shouting at the top of her voice: "I HATE EVERYONE!" But suddenly, just near her stamping feet, she saw a little furry head with long ears.

She stopped carrying on, and said: "Oh! A hare in my orchard!"

She didn't know whether to be pleased or annoyed, but as usual she chose to be annoyed. "You're trespassing, Hare! Go away at once."

"Oh, all right," said the hare. "If you prefer to be alone." And he hopped off.

"Wait!" cried the queen imperiously. The hare stopped and looked back. "I didn't know you could talk. That makes a difference. Come back and talk to me." She was used to ordering everyone about, but the hare didn't move.

"Come here, I said!" shouted the spoilt queen, stamping her foot.

"'Please' would be nice," said the hare.

"'PLEASE'!" echoed the queen. "A queen doesn't have to say 'please'!" The mere idea shocked her.

"Well, I don't know much about queens, but personally I don't like talking to *anyone* who doesn't say please. *And* thank you," said the hare very reasonably.

"You impertinent little animal!" cried the queen. "Do you presume to teach me manners?"

"Not at all," said the hare. "I don't care how you behave. All I said was that 'please' would be nice. Because I like things nice."

And he made off in great bounds, ignoring the queen's shouts at him to come back immediately.

That night the queen summoned her gamekeeper.

"There's a hare in the orchard," she said. "I want him for the pot. Shoot him."

The gamekeeper trembled in his boots.

"That hare can't be shot, Your Majesty," he muttered. "He's a magic hare. If you try to shoot him, he vanishes."

"A magic hare! I should have guessed," said the queen. "Then trap him for me – I want him alive."

"He can't be trapped either, ma'am."

"Then how am I to get my hands on him? I want him for my very own magic hare!"

The gamekeeper shook his head. "Nothing to be done," he said.

"This is all your fault, you stupid man!" railed the queen. "It's your job to catch game for me! You're dismissed!"

The gamekeeper, who had five children to feed, went away sadly. There was a lot of unemployment among gamekeepers.

No sooner was he out of the door than the hare appeared in front of the throne. The queen was so surprised that she jumped.

"How can you be so mean?" he asked indignantly.

"I do as I like! I'm the queen!" screamed the queen.

"More's the pity, if you ask me," muttered the hare.

"*What's that you said?*"

"I said, more's the pity. I should think your subjects would rather have almost any other queen than you."

The queen's mouth fell open. She was speechless. She had never in her whole life been spoken to like that, not even by her nanny when she was little.

The hare didn't take advantage

of her speechlessness to tell her off some more. Instead he did a little dance.

This had an extraordinary effect on the queen. It calmed her down. She sat watching the hare leaping about and her heartbeat slowed, her eyes lost their anger, and her fists unclenched.

Then something very strange happened. She found she had got to her feet and begun dancing, too, jumping and kicking her legs about just like the hare. Fortunately there was no one watching or they would have thought it very undignified.

The hare finished his dance. The

queen stopped too, breathless.

"I'm quite thirsty after that!" said the hare cheerfully. "Could you fancy a glass of water?"

"Water? I don't drink—" began the queen faintly. But before she could go on to say she never drank anything less than champagne, she found a glass of water in her hand,

and, feeling suddenly very thirsty, she drank some.

It was perfectly delicious! The most satisfying, cooling, thirst-quenching drink she'd ever drunk.

"This is divine!" she cried, and drank the lot. "Lovely and fizzy! Can you make this drink whenever you like?"

"Yes, but so can you. It comes from the spring in your garden."

"I'll never drink anything else!" said the queen. "I feel so good! What can I do to express what I feel?"

"You know," said the hare, and vanished.

The queen sat down and gave the

213

matter some thought.

Then she rang the bell and summoned her chancellor.

"Good morning, my dear Chancellor!" she said.

The poor man nearly fainted.

"I have some instructions for you, *please*, if you would be so very kind. First, call back my gamekeeper and ask him if he would stay in my employ – at double the wages, of course. Next, I am going to open my palace grounds for one day every month and give an enormous fête. Everyone's invited."

"Everyone, ma'am? You mean, *ordinary* people?"

214

"They're not ordinary people, they're my people. No expense to be spared. Especially for music. I want the best musicians, who specialize in music to dance to."

"Your commands shall be obeyed, Your Majesty," said the astounded chancellor, bowing low.

"Not commands," said the queen. "Requests. Thank you, Chancellor, that will be all."

The chancellor backed out of the room in the approved manner, but he was in such a state that he tripped and fell over backwards.

The queen helped him up.

"I'm so very, humbly sorry, Your

Majesty—" began the chancellor, all of a tremble.

"Entirely my fault," said the queen.

Greedy Gregory's Tooth

Nan McNab

Greedy Gregory's tooth had been loose for days. At school, while he was meant to be learning his tables, Greedy Gregory pushed at the tooth with his tongue. When he ate his lunch he would bite down hard on his choo-choo bar, hoping that the tooth would come out. It did get stuck in a lump of Jersey toffee once, but Greedy Gregory was too scared to tug it out – he had to wait half an hour for the toffee to dissolve.

Walking home from school, he twisted the tooth back and forth with his dirty fingers but, even though it was only hanging by a thread, it still wouldn't come out.

Then late one afternoon, his sister caught him by surprise with a kung fu kick to the jaw. He was just about to counter-attack when he felt the tooth – it was lying on his tongue, just behind his bottom teeth, and there was a big spongy lump where his tooth used to be.

"Maaam, Daaad!" he yelled.

"You sook!" said his little sister.

"I hardly touched you . . ."

But Greedy Gregory pushed past her and ran into the kitchen.

"Mum! Dad! Look at me toof. What a beauty!"

Greedy Gregory's dad took down a glass and filled it up with water. "Put your tooth in that," he said, "and we'll see what the tooth fairy brings you tonight."

Greedy Gregory dropped the tooth into the glass of water and held it up to the light. The tooth looked even bigger through the glass.

"A toof like that must be worth at least a dollar," said Greedy Gregory.

219

"Don't be funny," said his dad. "You'll be lucky to get five cents for it – it's got a great big hole in it. Not to mention the colour."

Greedy Gregory scowled at his dad. "That toof fairy had better give me a dollar or I'll smash 'er," he said, and he went off to the bathroom to count the rest of his teeth. His sister followed him and watched while he stood in front of the mirror and opened his mouth wide. It was not a pretty sight. All his teeth were green or grey, and bits of his lunch were still stuck in the gaps.

"Un, ooo, eee, or, ive, ix . . ." Greedy Gregory counted all his

teeth, top and bottom – incisors, canine teeth and molars – then he multiplied by a dollar (the one-times table was the only one he could remember).

"I'll be rich!" he cried. "Twenty dollars! Think of all the lollies I can buy with twenty dollars!" And he counted his teeth all over again, just to be sure.

"You won't get a dollar a tooth for those horrible green things," said his sister, and marched off to practise her karate.

"Just you wait and see," he yelled. "If I don't get a dollar a toof, that fairy'd better watch out," and he pulled his most ferocious face.

That night, Greedy Gregory went to bed extra early to wait for the tooth fairy. He put the glass of water on his bedside table and stared at the tooth. It did look a bit green in the lamplight. There was a dark brown hole in one side, but Greedy Gregory was sure it was worth more than five cents. It was such a *big* tooth, and besides, it was *his*.

I'll stay awake till the toof fairy comes, he thought, *and if she tries to leave me anything less than a dollar I'll* . . . yawn.

Greedy Gregory's eyes began to close, and his head sank onto his chest.

"*Ping!*" Something long and hard and springy landed on Gregory's head.

"Uh – what . . . ?" Greedy Gregory blinked. There was a funny blue light in the room. He rubbed his eyes.

"I said *ping*!"

Gregory looked up, and up, and up. The biggest tooth fairy he had ever seen was standing beside his bed, whacking him on the head with her wand.

"Are you Greedy Gregory?" she snapped.

"Yes I am."

"And this is your tooth?"

"Yes it is," said Greedy Gregory.

"Right," said the fairy, tucking her wand under her arm and plonking herself down on the bed. "How much do you want for it?"

Gregory wished she'd move over a bit – she was squashing his legs. His knees felt as if they might bend back the wrong way at any moment.

"Come on – don't muck about," said the fairy. "Do you know how many kids I have to see tonight?"

"I want a dollar," said Greedy Gregory.

"Nothing doing," said the fairy. "The going rate is five cents."

"Not for Gregory Grabham's teef," he replied firmly.

"Oh, indeed? Pardon me," said the fairy. "I thought we were talking about this nasty green object." The fairy prodded the tooth with her wand. "Gregory Grabham's *teeth*," she added, "are a different matter." And she began to do some quick calculations.

Greedy Gregory leant back on his pillow and watched the fairy filling in some figures in a little book. *Fairies are all the same*, he thought smugly, *treat them tough and they give you what you want*.

"This is the first tooth you've ever lost?" asked the fairy.

"Yes."

"So, counting this tooth, you've got twenty teeth altogether?"

"That's right," said Gregory. The fairy was obviously no fool – she knew how much she'd have to pay for a Gregory Grabham tooth. He began to imagine the sweets and ice creams he'd be able to buy tomorrow.

"Right," said the fairy, under her breath. "Twenty teeth at five cents a tooth makes a dollar." (The fairy knew her five-times table back to front.)

Greedy Gregory was so busy thinking of food that he only heard the last bit: ". . . a tooth makes a dollar".

"That's right," he said firmly. "I'll take nothing less than a dollar."

"All right," said the fairy, "a dollar it is. Sign here." And she held out the book for Gregory to sign with a special magic pencil that wrote everything in triplicate.

227

Greedy Gregory was so eager to get his dollar that he signed straight away without reading a word of the contract.

"Done!" said the fairy, shutting the book with a bang. "Now, open your mouth."

"What?" cried Gregory.

"Open your mouth!" said the fairy. "Don't muck about."

"Why should I?" said Greedy Gregory.

The fairy was getting impatient, and her face was getting redder and redder. "Look," she said, "we made a deal. You get your dollar and I get your teeth."

"My *what*?" squeaked Gregory.

"Your teeth, dumbskull. Now open your mouth."

Greedy Gregory went very pale. "But . . . but . . ." he stammered, "I thought it was a dollar a toof."

"Don't be wet," said the fairy. "A dollar for *that*! Look at it." She picked the tooth up gingerly between her finger and thumb, and held it under Gregory's nose. "It's *green*!" she snapped. "It hasn't been cleaned for *months*! And it's got a big ugly *hole* in one side. What use is a tooth like that?"

Greedy Gregory stared at his tooth. It didn't look too good, jammed between the fairy's big freckly fingers. A drop of dirty water fell off the end of the tooth and soaked into the sheet. Gregory began to cry.

"Now look here," said the fairy, "no crying – it was all fair and square. You want a dollar, right? At five cents a tooth, multiplied by twenty teeth, you get a dollar. Now I can't say fairer than that."

Gregory wished he'd practised his five-times table. His teacher was right – you never knew when you might need them.

The fairy reached into a bag she had slung over her back and pulled out an enormous pair of pliers. "Come on now," she said gruffly. "I can't muck around all night."

Greedy Gregory felt sick. "I don't want a dollar," he snivelled, staring at the huge pliers. "I want to keep my teef!"

The fairy waved the pliers at Gregory. "Look, kid – we made a deal and you signed it fair and square."

"But I want to un-make it," sobbed Gregory.

"Can't un-make a deal," said the fairy sternly. "All you can do is make a new one."

"Yes! Yes!" he cried. "Anything."

The fairy pulled out another book and flipped through the pages. "Well," she said, "You haven't got much to offer me –

unless your teeth improve a bit. Perhaps Form CT.20 might do the trick."

Greedy Gregory wiped his eyes and peered at the form. This time he read every word – even the fine print at the bottom of the page. Here is what it said:

> *I, ..., do solemnly swear to take good care of all my teeth, to visit the dentist every six months, and to brush my teeth after every meal.*
> *Signed ....*

And in the small print at the bottom:

I also promise not to eat too many lollies or ice creams or sweet biscuits.

Gregory signed.

Next morning, Gregory woke late. His eyes were all puffy and he felt awful. He ran his tongue over his teeth. Thank goodness – they were all there, just as furry and dirty as they were last night. He raced into the bathroom and grabbed a toothbrush.

"Did you look in your tooth glass?" asked his mum as he scrubbed away at his teeth. "The tooth fairy left you something."

Gregory walked slowly back into

his room. There on the sheet was the dirty mark where the tooth fairy had dropped a little water the night before. Greedy Gregory hardly dared to look in the glass. What if there were a dollar coin at the bottom – would she come back another night with her pliers and pull out all his teeth?

But there at the bottom of the glass was a shiny silver five-cent coin.

"Look, Mum," said Gregory, "five cents!" And he gave his mother a big, white, gleaming smile.

Lindalou and her Golden Gift

Anna Fienberg

When Lindalou was born, her mother and father were surprised.

Her aunt fainted.

The cat's whiskers fell off.

For curled in each of Lindalou's little fists were two strange and beautiful things. In her right hand lay a tiny golden hammer. In her left lay a golden nail.

Lindalou was a quiet baby. She smiled when her mother filled her cradle with teddies and ducks and woolly tigers. But she didn't play with them.

Lindalou played only with her tiny golden hammer and tiny golden nail.

When a year had passed, Lindalou said her first word.

"Wood," she said, clear as a bell.

"Wood?" said her mother, puzzled. But off she went to the timber yard that lay at the edge of the forest. She chose for her daughter a piece from each and every kind of wood that she found there.

237

When another year had passed, Lindalou said her second words.

"More wood," she said, clear as a bell.

"More wood?" said her mother, puzzled.

"Yes," said Lindalou. "I want a piece of rosewood for its purple heart, a piece of sassafras for its tiger stripes, and a piece of satinwood because it is as fine and golden as my little hammer."

"But what are you going to make?" asked her mother.

"Something," said Lindalou, and smiled.

Lindalou was no longer a quiet baby. She hammered and sang, and sang and hammered. At the end of the first week she had made a box.

The box was the size of a duck's egg, and just as smooth. Its corners were as rounded as cheeks, and the satinwood glowed and rippled like the sun on water.

"She's really very good," said her mother, looking closely.

"She's really very loud," said her father, blocking his ears.

While Lindalou worked, someone was looking over her shoulder. His name was Aristan, and he came from a long line of magic spiders. Swinging there on the wall, he shone like a dab of butter, for he was as golden as

Linda's little hammer and nail.

"What will I put in the box?" Linda would ask herself each day.

"Secrets," Aristan would whisper.

Linda liked making boxes, and she liked having Aristan for company. Soon she was singing and hammering so loudly that her parents could not sleep. Her mother bought a set of earplugs. Her father wore a pillow around his head.

"For mercy's sake, get rid of the golden hammer!" shouted her aunt when she came to visit.

But how could they take away the golden gifts that came into the world with Lindalou?

By the end of the third week, Lindalou had made another two boxes. They were perfect, like the first, but different. One was made from sassafras, for its tiger stripes, and the other from rosewood, for its purple heart.

Lindalou was pleased with her boxes. She lined them up on the floor, next to her bed, so that she could look at them before she fell asleep.

That night, Linda dreamed of a house in the trees. It was shaped like a boat, moored between two branches. Lindalou stood at the window, steering her boathouse into an ocean of sky.

"Now I'll sail past the stars at night and hammer and sing amongst the trees by day," she said in her dream.

When Lindalou awoke the next morning, she bent down to look at her boxes. She picked the first one up and opened it.

Inside she found tiny golden tools! There was a saw for cutting wood, a clamp for holding wood in place, and a plane to smooth its edges. As she took out each piece, it began to shine and hum and grow until it was just the right size for her hand.

In the second box she found small pieces of wood: the ones she knew, and *new* kinds: ebony and silky oak and cedar. As she took them out, each piece began to shine and hum and grow until the whole room was filled with wood.

In the third box, Lindalou found a piece of paper rolled up and tied with golden threads. Inside was Aristan. He was moving quickly across the page, leaving a trail of fine spidery lines.

When he had finished, and Lindalou saw what he had made, she laughed with joy. There on the page was a plan of the house in her dream!

No one saw Lindalou – or Aristan – for a week. Her parents found a note tacked on her door: *Away on Business*.

The house was very quiet without Lindalou. Her mother took off her earplugs. Her father left his pillow on the bed. Even the cat's whiskers grew back.

"You can hear a pin drop, without Lindalou," said her mother.

"Who wants to hear a pin drop?" said her father. And off they went to find Lindalou.

Through the forest they walked, searching and calling, until they came to the timber yard.

"Have you seen a little girl pass this way?" they asked the man chopping wood.

"Yes," he said. "She was heading for the other side of the forest."

On they hurried now, along the twisting paths of the forest, calling "Lindalou! Linda . . . *lou*!" and as they ran, aunts and uncles, cousins and friends came to join them.

They drew near a stream, and a sound of singing and hammering filled the air.

"That's my girl!" cried her father, and they searched the long grasses and between the rocks, but still they couldn't find Lindalou.

Then a shout came down from the treetops. "Up here!" called a voice, and there, between the branches of a maple tree, perched the most magnificent house anyone had ever seen. And in the doorway, smiling at them all, was Lindalou.

"Come in!" she called.

So, up the rope stairs went her mother and father. Up climbed her aunt and uncle, her friends and the woodchopper. Last of all came the cat.

"Welcome to my new house," said Lindalou. "Here I can hammer and sing by day and sail past the stars at night." She looked over at Aristan, swinging there on the wall. "Tonight we are going to Kathmandu. Would anyone like to come?"

"*We* would!" cried her mother and father.

"*I* would!" said the woodchopper.

"How do we get there?" asked her aunt.

247

"Simple," replied Lindalou. "Do you see this steering wheel and the little lever? When I push the lever, the house rises up into the clouds, and this is how I steer."

"Are there any tigers in Kathmandu?" asked the woodchopper nervously. But only the cat was listening.

Everyone hurried home to fetch their pyjamas and toothbrushes and Lindalou opened her *Guide to Kathmandu*.

That evening, as the sun was setting, the birds of the forest saw a strange sight. A beautiful wooden house rose above the treetops and went sailing past. It was filled with smiling people and a startled cat, all waving from the windows, and a ripple of happy voices drifted back as the house became a tiny speck in the distance.

Atalanta's Race

A Greek Myth

Geraldine McCaughrean

On the island of Cyprus, in a
lovely garden tended by
Venus, the goddess of love, there
grew an apple tree. It had yellow
branches and yellow leaves, but its
apples were glittering gold.

Now, in the days when that tree
was in fruit, there lived a beautiful
girl called Atalanta. Men had only
to see her to fall in love with her,

but she had sworn never to marry. The young men pestered her to change her mind and grew tiresome. So she declared, "I will only marry the man who can race against me and *win*. But anyone who tries – and fails – must agree to die."

Despite the risk, many young men wanted to race Atalanta to win her hand. But she could run like the wind. The runners tried and the runners died, because they came in second.

A young man named Hippomenes had heard of Atalanta's races. He thought any boy must be stupid to throw his life away on a silly dare. But when one day Atalanta streaked by him, brown and fast as a darting bird, he knew at once that he had to race for her.

When Atalanta saw Hippomenes, she did not want him to challenge her. He was too young and

handsome to die. She half wanted him to win . . . but no! She had sworn never to marry.

A crowd gathered, impatient for another race, but Atalanta kept them waiting as she fretted about the result. And Hippomenes said his prayers.

"Oh, Venus!" prayed Hippomenes. "You plainly made me love this woman. So help me to win her!"

Venus heard him. She also thought Hippomenes too young and handsome to die. So she picked from the tree her garden three golden apples and gave them to him. Now he was ready for the race.

*

"*Ready, steady, go!*" cried the starter.

Away went Hippomenes, as fast as he had ever run. Away went Atalanta, quick as a blink. She soon took the lead.

So Hippomenes threw one golden apple – beyond her, over her head. It caught the light. Atalanta ran to where it lay and picked it up. Hippomenes sped ahead.

But Atalanta caught him up again and passed him, hair blowing like a flag. He ran faster than any of the other suitors, but it was not fast enough.

So Hippomenes threw another of

the apples. Again Atalanta stopped to pick it up and again Hippomenes took the lead. But Atalanta was so much faster that she could stop, admire, pick up the shiny apples and *still* catch him up again.

Hippomenes ran faster than any man has ever run, but it was not fast enough. So he threw the third apple. Would Atalanta be fooled by the trick a third time? She saw . . . she slowed down . . . she glanced at the two apples in her hands . . . And she stopped for the third. The crowd cheered as Hippomenes dashed past her, lungs bursting, and threw himself over the winning line. He had won his bride!

And for a champion runner who has just lost a race for the first time Atalanta looked extremely happy.

ACKNOWLEDGEMENTS

The publishers wish to thank the following for permission to reproduce copyright material:

Anna Fienberg: "Lindalou and her Golden Gift" from *The Magnificent Nose and Other Marvels* by Anna Fienberg; first published by Allen and Unwin Pty Ltd and reproduced with their permission.

Naomi Adler: "The Dragon and the Cockerel" from *Barefoot Book of Animal Tales* by Naomi Adler; first published by Barefoot Books 1996 and reproduced with their permission.

Bookmart Ltd: "The Musicians of Bremen" from *Fairy Tales from the Brothers Grimm*; first published by Bookmart Ltd 1997 and reproduced with their permission.

Phillippa Pearce: "The Great Sharp Scissors" and "The Manatee" from *The Lion at School and Other Stories* by Phillippa Pearce; first published by Viking Kestrel and © Phillippa Pearce 1971; reproduced by permission of the Laura Cecil Literary Agency.

V.H. Drummond: "The Flying Postman"; reproduced by permission of V.H. Drummond Productions.

David L. Harrison: "The Little Boy's Secret" from *The Book of Giant Stories* by David Harrison; first published by Jonathan Cape 1972 and reproduced with their permission.

Joan Aiken: "Clem's Dream" from *The Last Slice of Rainbow and Other Stories* by Joan Aiken; © Joan Aiken Enterprises Ltd 1985; reproduced by permission of A.M. Heath & Co Ltd on behalf of the author.

Berlie Doherty: "The Sandboat" from *Round About Six*, compiled by Kaye Webb; first published by Frances Lincoln Ltd 1992; reproduced by permission of David Higham Associates on behalf of the author.

Ruth Manning-Sanders: "The Fat Grandmother"; reproduced by permission of David Higham Associates on behalf of the author.

Nan McNab: "Greedy Gregory's Tooth" from *The Macquarie Bedtime Story Book*.

Margaret Mahy: "The Man Whose Mother was a Pirate" from *A Lion in the Meadow* by Margaret Mahy; first published by Orion Children's Books 1976 and reproduced with their permission.

Andrew Matthews: "The Hobyahs" from *Silly Stories* by Andrew Matthews; first published by Orion Children's Books 1994 and reproduced with their permission.

Lance Salway: "The Boy Who Wasn't Bad Enough" from *Bad Boys*; first published by Puffin Books and © Lance Salway 1972; reproduced by permission of Rogers Coleridge & White Ltd on behalf of the author.

Lynne Reid Banks: "The Hare and the Spoilt Queen" from *Twelve Stories of the Magic Hare*; first published by HarperCollins 1992 and reproduced by permission of Watson, Little Limited on behalf of the author.

Rose Impey: "The Three Wishes" from *The Orchard Book of Fairy Tales* by Rose Impey; first published by Orchard Books 1992 and reproduced by permission of The Watts Publishing Group.

Geraldine McCaughrean: "Atalanta's Race" from *The Orchard Book of Greek Myths* by Geraldine McCaughrean; first published by Orchard Books 1992 and reproduced by permission of The Watts Publishing Group.

Every effort has been made to trace the copyright holders but where this has not been possible or where any error has been made the publishers will be pleased to make the necessary arrangement at the first opportunity.

Funny stories

for **6** year olds

Chosen by Helen Paiba

A bright and varied selection of wonderfully entertaining stories by some of the very best writers for children. Perfect for reading alone or aloud – and for dipping into time and time again. With stories from Margaret Mahy, David Henry Wilson, Francesca Simon, Tony Bradman and many more, this book will provide hours of fantastic fun.

Animal Stories

for 6 year olds

Chosen by Helen Paiba

A bright and varied selection of
heart-warming animal stories by some
of the very best writers for children.
Perfect for reading alone or aloud – and for
dipping into time and time again.
With stories from David Henry Wilson,
Meredith Hooper, Dick King-Smith,
Margaret Mahy and many more, this book
will provide hours of fantastic fun.

Bedtime stories

for **6** year olds

Chosen by Helen Paiba

Snuggle up with this cosy and varied
selection of stories for bedtime by some
of the very best writers for children.
Perfect for reading alone or aloud –
and for dipping into time and time again.
With stories from Rudyard Kipling,
Joan Aiken, Dick King-Smith, Malorie
Blackman and many more, this book will
provide perfect bedtime reading.